FORBIDDEN ...

"I've just been to the Judenrat," the doctor announced. "They sent for me to tell me about von Holtzer's latest . . . something that concerns you too, that's why I felt I should talk to you tonight—

"Tomorrow . . . ," he began and paused. "Tomorrow it will be posted on the walls: HENCEFORTH PREGNANCIES WILL BE FORBIDDEN IN THE GHETTO."

He'd said it, and now he looked straight at them. They sat in stunned silence, looking back at him in disbelief. Finally Hershel said, "Henceforth. *But what about those that are already pregnant?*"

ON THE OTHER SIDE OF THE GATE

A NOVEL BY

YURI SUHL

AVON
PUBLISHERS OF BARD, CAMELOT, DISCUS, EQUINOX AND FLARE BOOKS

This book is dedicated to the memory
of the 1,200,000 Jewish children who perished
at the hands of the Nazis in the ghettos and death camps
of occupied Europe.

Though this book was inspired
by an actual episode it was
conceived as a work of fiction
and should be read as such.

AVON BOOKS
A division of
The Hearst Corporation
959 Eighth Avenue
New York, New York 10019

Copyright © 1975 by Yuri Suhl.
Published by arrangement with Franklin Watts, Inc.
Library of Congress Catalog Card Number: 74-13452

ISBN: 0-380-00854-8

First Avon Printing, November, 1976

AVON TRADEMARK REG. U.S. PAT. OFF. AND IN
OTHER COUNTRIES, MARCA REGISTRADA,
HECHO EN U.S.A.

Printed in the U.S.A.

PART ONE

1

ON THE MORNING of September 1, 1939, the town awoke to the news that Hitler's army had crossed the Polish frontier. "POLAND INVADED!" read a banner headline in the *Gazette & Courier,* the town's only newspaper. And right below it, in smaller print: "Government Declares State of Emergency. Country Mobilizes To Repel Enemy Assault. Warsaw Mayor Urges Calm. Calls on Citizens To Erect Barricades."

On that day the town square was crowded with clusters of people, milling about restlessly, buzzing with talk. And at the water pump, which stood in the middle of the square, those who had already filled their cans were standing around to talk to those who were still waiting their turn at the pump. It was all speculation, of course. No one was any wiser than his neighbor. Still, there was the need to hear what others had to say. And when they had talked themselves out and realized that it was getting late, that they had work to do, they went home and others took their place.

Only Mendel, the water carrier, would not tarry at the pump. He had no time to waste on talk. He had deliveries to make. As soon as his cans were full he was on his way, his short, heavy-set figure stooped from the weight of the full cans hanging from the wooden yoke on his shoulders, moving ponderously through the town's muddy, unpaved streets, as though it were just another day in his life, a day that ended at sundown, in time to go to the synagogue for evening prayers.

But his own customers did slow him down a bit that day by impinging on his time. *"Nu,* Reb Mendel," they would ask, "what do you say to the news?" Not that they expected enlightenment from a water carrier. But there was danger in the air. Hitler—may his name be erased—was pouring his hordes into Poland. In such times a Jew was eager for a word of comfort from a fellow Jew, be he even a water carrier.

"What's there to say?" Mendel would shrug. "We have a great Father in heaven and He will not abandon us. In my lifetime I have seen them come and go—the Cossacks, the Denikins, the Petluras. Now it's the Germans. We've survived our enemies then and we'll survive them now." The need to believe in Mendel's words was so strong that at that moment at least they endowed this simple water carrier with the powers of a prophet. And to the hope raised by this pious Jew they added their own—the world. The world, they would tell themselves and each other, will not stand idly by and let this madman swallow up Poland. Because if it does, other countries will be next. For its own protection the world must stop him in his tracks.

In the meantime German tanks kept rolling deeper into Poland and German planes kept raining bombs over Warsaw to soften the city for surrender, while the world applauded the citizens of the Polish capital for their brave stand behind the barricades.

The world applauded and Warsaw fell. And Lodz. And Cracow. And all the other towns and villages that lay in the path of the invader's onward sweep. And one morning, late in September, a detachment of the Wehrmacht, headed by a large tank flying a black swastika, goosestepped into the town and took it without firing a single shot. The tank came to a halt in the middle of the square, a few feet away from the water pump.

Soon the square was filled to overflowing with people who had run out of their homes to catch a glimpse of the helmeted conquerors. Those at the water pump were trapped. Somehow Mendel had managed to leave with his full cans while it was still possible. People paused to stare at this odd Jew going about his business as though nothing momentous was

7

happening in town. Everyone was hurrying to the square and he was going away from it!

To Jews who stayed home that morning behind bolted doors and peered out the window through a crack in the parted curtain the familiar sight of the water carrier with his two full cans provided a momentary sense of comfort. If Mendel was out there making deliveries, maybe things were not so bad after all.

On the square a military band struck up "Deutschland Über Alles," while the soldiers and officers stood at attention. When the playing was over Major Kurt von Holtzer, a tall, wiry man in his early forties, stepped from a gray, open-top car. A young blond-haired lieutenant appeared at his side. The major adjusted the pince-nez on his rather long, pointed nose and let his eyes roam through the crowd until a hush fell over the square. Then he pulled a piece of paper from his coat pocket and, in a high-pitched, almost shrill voice, read from it in German, pausing now and then for the lieutenant to translate into Polish:

I greet you in the name of the Fuhrer and the Third Reich. At this moment I have two important announcements. One: All weapons and ammunition and all shortwave radios now in the hands of private citizens must be turned over to the occupation authorities within three days. Failure to comply with this order is punishable by death. Two: I hereby declare a curfew, commencing at 8 P.M. and ending at 5 A.M. Anyone found in the street during curfew hours without a special permit from the proper authorities will be summarily shot.
All further announcements will be posted on the walls in both German and Polish.
Those who obey the orders of the occupation authorities have nothing to fear.
That will be all for now.

There was no applause and the silence continued until after the major reentered the car and drove off.

In the meantime Mendel had returned to the square. He'd remained standing at the edge of the crowd and when the major had begun to speak he had cupped his right ear and strained to listen. What the German was saying did not apply to him, Mendel thought. He had no weapons to give up and no radio and he made no deliveries after sundown. By eight o'clock he was usually getting ready for bed.

The solid mass, locked in frozen silence a moment ago, now heaved and swayed and hummed with talk. Mendel, gripping his cans by their ears, moved sideways as he inched toward the pump. When he finally got to it there were others ahead of him. He took his place in line, surveying the scene while he waited.

He watched the soldiers mingling freely with the people, flirting with the girls and handing out chocolate to the children. It was the same in 1914, he recalled. When the Cossacks took the town they also flirted with the girls and passed out biscuits to the children. Later they raped Jewish women and looted Jewish stores. Then, at least, the Jews could look forward to the Kaiser's army to drive out the Czar's. But who will drive out Hitler's devils? he wondered.

"Your turn," the man behind him broke into his thoughts, "what are you waiting for?"

Indeed, what was he waiting for, the Messiah? With a heavy heart he picked up an empty can and placed it under the pump's mouth. He had more comforting words for his customers than for himself.

And he would not be stampeded into pumping any faster than usual because the Germans had taken the town and caused a crowd to gather around the pump. After thirty years as a water carrier he had his own way of drawing water from the depth of the earth. His left foot planted forward, his massive hand wrapped around the iron handle, he bore down on it with effortless ease and a stream rushed from the pump's mouth. Back and forth his body moved in slow, deliberate

9

rhythm, as though he were swaying in prayer. And he stopped just in time. He never pumped to overflow. For that would be a waste of the earth's gift.

Just as Mendel had pulled the full can from under the pump someone knocked the cap off his head with such force that it landed a few feet away from him. Startled, he wheeled about, scanning the ground, his left hand covering his head. He was a pious Jew and would not, if he could help it, for one moment be bareheaded. He spotted his cap and was about to retrieve it when a tall, sandy-haired youth beat him to it.

"Here, you scabby-head Jew," the youth dangled the cap tauntingly in front of Mendel. "Here, take it." But the instant Mendel reached for it the youth tossed it to his buddy, a pimple-faced boy of about sixteen. He held it until Mendel came close to him then threw it back to his friend. And so the cap was passed from one to the other like a ball while the crowd roared with laughter. In the meantime several soldiers had climbed to the top of the tank and trained their cameras on the scene.

Mendel realized that it was hopeless; that he would never get his cap back. So why provide the goyim with a spectacle for their amusement? Why make yourself the butt of their laughter? But neither did he want to walk through the streets with his head bare, like a Gentile. "God is my witness that it is not my fault," he said to himself. He would fill the other can, walk straight home, find another cap, even if it be the one he wore on the Sabbath, and continue with his deliveries.

He was about to reach for the empty can when he heard a voice coming from behind him: "Why don't you give him back his cap? You ought to be ashamed of yourself, taunting a man for nothing." It was an elderly, frail-looking woman, wrapped in a black shawl that covered her head and framed her small, bird-like face.

"Mind your business you old, Jew-lovin' hag," one

10

of the boys retorted, sticking his tongue out at the woman.

"You behave like a hooligan and you talk like one. Give the man back his cap, I say!" She trembled all over, as though she had drawn her voice from every ounce of herself; and for an instant her command hung in the air like an ominous threat, directed not only at the youth but at everyone in the crowd. For an instant even those who a moment ago had tittered and laughed, seemed uncertain of themselves.

"Here, you give it to him," the boy said, holding up the cap, as though ready to relinquish it. The woman began to move toward him, her hand outstretched, while his friend trailed quietly behind her. The boy let her approach him within an arm's length of himself before the cap became a ball again, flying back and forth over the woman's head until a man, wearing a railwayman's cap and coat, appeared as if from nowhere and caught the cap in midair.

The two youths were about to lunge at him but something held them back. Perhaps it was the uniform. Any uniform, even a railwayman's, commanded a certain awe. Or perhaps it was the man's look. It seemed to say: "Just try and see what'll happen." They didn't dare. They muttered a few obscenities under their breath and slunk away to the edge of the crowd.

The railwayman handed Mendel his cap and said, "Take my advice, pick up your cans and go. These hoodlums are out for trouble."

"Thank you kindly," Mendel said, pulling the cap firmly down on his head to secure it against further mishaps. "I'll just fill up the other can."

"Go now," the man urged. "If I were you, I'd get away from here as fast as possible."

It pained Mendel to have to empty a full can of water on the ground. It was like committing a sin. But the man was right. He should leave at once. Right now this was no place for a Jew. For the first time in all his years as a water carrier he walked away from the pump with empty cans.

With nothing to weigh him down he could easily have run, at least quickened his pace, but he chose to move with the same slow, deliberate steps as always. Empty cans or full, Mendel is not running. That satisfaction he will not give them. He was nearing the tank. In a minute he would be past it and out of the square. Where was his next delivery? He couldn't remember. Well, what difference did it make? He had nothing to deliver anyway. If the cans were full, they would lead him there on their own . . .

"Jude! Stehen bleiben!" one of the soldiers on the tank shouted down to him. Mendel walked on. A dog barks, let him bark. A soldier emerged from the crowd and blocked his path. "When a German gives a command you obey, you Jew pig," the soldier barked at Mendel and slapped his face. Mendel stood there motionless, his eyes fixed on the German, his right hand clutching hard the ear of the empty can to keep from striking back. Should he go now, or wait till he was ordered to? He decided to wait. Why give this anti-Semite the excuse to slap him again?

"Schneid ihm den Bart ab," a soldier on the tank called down.

"Ja, ja," the others nodded, pointing to their chins.

The soldier facing Mendel pulled the bayonet from its sheath and with his left hand grabbed Mendel's beard. With one yank of the head Mendel pulled his beard free, leaving a clump of hair in the German's fist. He stepped away but the soldier grabbed him by the coat and pulled him back. "Not so fast, Jew. Not before you get your trim." He seized the beard and tightened his grip around it. He was about to cut when one of the soldiers with a camera called down from the tank: *"Langsam, langsam."* The soldier below acknowledged the request with a wink and a nod and began to move the bayonet slowly over Mendel's reddish beard back and forth, like a saw, while the cameras were clicking away.

Some in the crowd made their way a little closer to the scene. A Jew's beard had always been a tempting target for a pull and a yank but few dared to actually clip one. Now it was about to happen in front of their eyes. A sight not to be missed.

Maybe it's only a game they're playing, a thought occurred to Mendel. What do they need my beard for? They only want pictures of another soldier cutting a Jew's beard. That's why they're so busy with the cameras up there. All right. Let him fiddle away with the bayonet. Let them have their pictures. So long as they leave my beard alone. As for the laughter from the crowd . . . a dog barks, let him bark. He decided to stand still until the joke was over and he would be on his way.

Suddenly the soldier stopped fiddling and began to use the beyonet in earnest. He gripped the beard closer to the chin and pulled it so taut that the hair yielded even to a dull blade. "No! Not the beard!" Mendel cried out. He was a Jew and the beard was part of it. Like observing the Sabbath, or going to the synagogue. He couldn't imagine himself without his beard. He grabbed the German by the wrist and twisted his arm with such force that the bayonet fell from his hand.

A murmur swept through the crowd. The soldiers in crouched position on the tank sprang to their feet. One of them put down his camera and whipped out his pistol. He took aim at Mendel and fired. For a moment Mendel stood there, staring up at the soldier who shot him, as though he were defying death. Then he keeled over backward and fell on the cobblestone pavement with the full impact of his hulking body. He lay motionless, framed by his two empty cans and his wooden yoke; his eyes half open, his beard half cut, his cap still under his head.

The crowd stood still, as though too stunned to move. The woman who had come to Mendel's defense now stepped up close to his body and viewed it with grieving eyes. "Jesus, Maria," she muttered, crossing herself, then turned and walked away. Wrapped in her black shawl she looked like a figure in mourning.

The soldier on the ground picked up his bayonet

and, with one push of the palm, jammed it back into the sheath. The soldier on the tank put his pistol back in the holster and reached for his camera. He leaned forward, training the lens on the corpse for one more shot.

2

SOMETIME around the middle of November a rumor began circulating in town that von Holtzer had a plan to put all the Jews into a ghetto. It was to happen any day now. Days passed and it didn't happen. But the rumor persisted.

Rumors were nothing new to the Jews. A Jew awoke every morning to a new rumor and by the time he went to bed it had multiplied to half a dozen. The rumors were spawned by his uncertain existence under German occupation. And although not all the rumors materialized, so many official anti-Jewish decrees had been preceded by rumors that no Jew could afford to take a rumor lightly.

But this one about the ghetto was particularly alarming to the Jews because if it should prove to be true it would mean the loss of the one anchor of stability in their precarious lives—their homes. Even though every knock on the door, every sound of an unfamiliar footstep in the hallway filled one with panic, ending the day in one's own home, sitting down at one's own table, sleeping in one's own bed, gave one a sense of security that allowed for a hope for better times. But a ghetto! It would be the first step into exile.

When questioned about the rumor the *Judenrat*, the Jewish Council appointed by von Holtzer, was evasive: "When we will know, you will know."

"And in the meantime?"

"In the meantime go about your business."

Some took this to mean that they did know. These were Jews who mistrusted the *Judenrat*. They looked upon it as a tool of the Germans, von Holtzer's errand boys. "A decent Jew should have no truck with these

Nazi henchmen," they said, and pointed to the rabbi and Dr. Weiss, director of the Jewish hospital, both of whom declined to join the *Judenrat*.

But not all were that critical of the twelve-man body, headed by the lawyer, Mauricy Gewirtzer, an assimilated Jew. These were difficult times, they argued, and they would rather deal with the Germans through fellow Jews than deal with them directly. As an example they pointed out that Jews were no longer being nabbed off the streets for forced labor. Under the new procedure the Germans requested from the *Judenrat* a certain number of Jews daily, and the *Judenrat* saw to it that the quota was filled. Now wasn't this a better arrangement than before?

"True," the critics retorted, "but who benefits from it? Those whose names never appear on the forced labor roster because they can afford to buy or bribe their way off it, or because they know the right people? As always the poor and the helpless carry the main burden." Clearly, the majority of the Jews were critical of the *Judenrat*.

In the meantime all kinds of speculations arose. Some were convinced that the rumor had been planted by certain Poles in order to panic the Jews into selling their belongings quickly and cheaply. Therefore, they said, they would not budge; they would not play into the Germans' hands. Others went by the simple rule that where there's smoke there's fire, and began selling off some of their furniture and other expensive things. Why let it fall into the hands of the Germans? Logic dictated that in such uncertain times cash and jewelry were the most practical possessions. You can sew them into your clothing and carry them on your body wherever you go. But on the other hand . . . there was always an "on the other hand," depending on whom you talked to.

One day, during those uncertain days, a young man named Hershel Bregman, wearing the compulsory Star of David on his sleeve, came home from work and found his wife, Lena, in tears. It was not the first time. Every day brought new decrees designed to make life more difficult for the Jews, and the hospital where Lena worked as nurse was no exception. One day all Jewish members of the hospital's Board of Directors were dismissed and replaced by Poles. Another day Dr. Weiss, who for years had been chief of staff, was removed from that post and was now taking orders from a Polish physician nearly half his age. Furthermore, he was forbidden to treat Aryan patients except by special permission from the German doctor on von Holtzer's staff, who was the real boss of the hospital. The same rule applied to Lena who, though a senior nurse, could serve Aryan patients only in the capacity of orderly.

"What happened?" Hershel asked. "What did they think up today?"

To his surprise Lena said, "It's not about the hospital. It's about me."

"About you? I don't understand."

"Dr. Weiss gave me a checkup and he suggested that I have an abortion."

"Anything wrong with the pregnancy?"

"No," she said, shaking her head. "It's not the pregnancy. It's the times we live in," and she burst into tears again.

He sat down near her, took her hand into his and stroked it smoothly. "Tell me exactly what he told you, Lena," he said.

"He told me, 'If I were you, I would think twice before bringing a new life into the world in times like these. Two months ago, when you learned you were pregnant, things were already pretty bad, but they were not *that* bad. An infant needs nourishment. The right kind of nourishment. That goes for the mother as well. And the Germans are bent on starving us to death. And it's not just the food. Men are being dragged off for forced labor and disappear. Women have become widows overnight, and children have become orphans overnight. God knows what will happen when they push us into a ghetto and cut us off from the world altogether. Then it might be too late for an abortion. That's why I say, do it now. You're both young. The war will not last forever. Have your children in better times.'" She fell silent and, after a long pause, nodded thoughtfully and said, "The trouble is he's right. I've been carrying around such thoughts with me for a long time."

"So you said yes?"

"I did not!" she said, resolutely, as though resenting his question. "I said I'd have to talk it over with my husband."

"And how do you feel about it now?"

"Do you have to ask? I don't want an abortion. I want the baby."

"If that's your decision, then it's also mine."

She clasped his hand and held it to her cheek, as though warming herself with it. "Thanks," she said in a low voice. "Now it will be easier to say no."

Their decision buoyed them both, gave them a sense of strength, even a sense of defiance. It was as though they were two young Jews standing up to Hitler and saying to him: "You will not take our child from us. That satisfaction you will not have!"

Later they returned to the subject. They had to assure themselves that their decision was not made lightly. They had to buttress it with a sober analysis of their situation. They considered their age (she was twenty-three, he twenty-six), a vital factor in the endurance of hardships. They discussed the merits of their respective occupations and here, too, the picture looked a little brighter for them than for many other Jews in town. While lawyers and teachers could no longer practice their professions, he and Lena were still able to work at their own skills. And he did not have to bribe his way off the forced labor roster either. As soon as the Germans discovered that he was a master electrician they transferred him from a forced labor battalion to a building project, the construction of a new headquarters for von Holtzer and his staff. Now

18

he carried in his pocket a *Facharbeiter Ausweis,* issued by the *Arbeitsamt,* which said that he was a skilled worker. It was a much coveted piece of paper because it protected its bearer from being picked off the street for some work detail whenever it suited the whim of a German soldier.

"And what'll happen when the building is finished?" Lena asked.

"There'll be other construction jobs. I hear the Germans are planning to put up a whole row of barracks just outside of town. Apparently they're settling in for a long stay."

They wondered what life would be like in a ghetto, if they had to be in one. Where would they be living? Would they be able to take their furniture with them? Would there be some kind of medical facility, if not a hospital, at least a clinic? They could only speculate about these matters, but of one thing they were certain: There would always be the need for a good nurse and a good electrician, especially one who could also do a little carpentry. And if Dr. Weiss would be with them in the ghetto the delivery would be in good hands. So all things considered there was no reason to regret their decision.

Suddenly he put his arm around her and said, excitedly, "I got an idea."

"What?"

"Let's buy a crib."

"A crib, now?" she laughed, "There's plenty of time for that."

"Dantziger's furniture sale is now. I hear he's giving away things for practically nothing."

"After Yom Kippur he still has merchandise left to sell?"

The mention of Yom Kippur never failed to evoke a moment of solemn silence. Not because it was the Day of Atonement, the holiest of all Jewish holidays, but because it conjured up a frightening vision that haunted the memory of every Jew in this town. For on that day, when the synagogue was crammed full of fasting

Jews, praying more fervently than ever, pleading more tearfully than ever with the One Above to come to their aid in this hour of their greatest misfortune; to assuage their sufferings; to liberate them from the new Haman, Hitler, may his name and memory be erased; on that day the Germans had instigated a pogrom.

It began with the looting of Jewish stores and ended with the beating, maiming, and even killing of Jews. Around eleven in the morning, when the looting was in full swing, six SS men stormed into the synagogue, picked fifty Jews, including the rabbi, and marched them off to the square in their prayer shawls and skullcaps. There they handed them each a broom and ordered them to sweep the square. When a gentile came to the pump for water, one of the Jews had to lay down the broom and pump the water for him.

Mordecai Dantziger, whose furniture store was on the square, was one of the fifty Jews. While sweeping the cobblestones, he could see his merchandise being carried off and he could do nothing about it. Polish police and German soldiers saw to it that there was no interfering with the looters.

Since that Yom Kippur Jews were reluctant to attend synagogue even on the Sabbath. Services were held in various private homes.

"They overlooked the basement," Hershel replied. They probably didn't know about it. I suppose now, with this ghetto rumor in the air, he's trying to salvage what he can."

"And who's buying furniture these days? Gentiles, I suppose."

"Jews too. Either they don't believe there'll be a ghetto, or they can't resist a bargain."

"You think it's wise for us to invest in a crib at this time?"

"What have we got to lose? A few zlotys? He's selling out. So let's get it while we can."

"All right. Let's buy one."

Lena now looked at peace with herself, as though the decision to buy a crib had wiped away the last

20

lingering doubts she may have had about going through with the pregnancy.

The next day Hershel went straight from work to Dantziger's. When he got to the square, he had to pause a moment to get his bearings. There were so many boarded-up show windows along the same row of stores that at a first glance he couldn't tell them apart. By tearing down the signs over the stores the looters made them all anonymous. The owners' individual names were now merged in a single word: JUDE, the German-inspired racial graffiti that appeared all over town on store windows whole or smashed, on walls and doors of Jewish homes, even on sidewalks, scrawled in white chalk or paint. Illiterates who had trouble signing their own name overnight became proficient in the spelling of a foreign word.

He remembered when Lena made both their armbands. She had to work late into the night because they had to conform to precise measurements and the word JUDE had to be sewn in neatly in the very center of the Star of David. When she'd finished and both tried them on, she had said, "From now on we'll be on public display, like animals in a zoo."

"It'll not be the first time," he remembered telling her. "The Germans are not even original in this. They borrowed the idea from anti-Semites of the past. The Romans. The Poles . . ."

"The Romans? The Poles?" she had looked at him questioningly.

"Yes. As far back as the thirteenth century, at the time of the crusades, Christian leaders had decreed that Jews must wear some kind of badge on their clothing to mark them as outcasts. Three centuries later one of the popes improved on that decree. Not only were the Jews of Rome compelled to wear yellow hats, but they were also forced to live in a ghetto."

"Does that mean that after the armband comes the ghetto?"

"Could very well be."

21

"And when did it happen in Poland?"

"Also in the sixteenth century. In Piotrkow the Jews were not allowed to dress like Christians, and in addition they had to wear yellow hats and badges so that they could be identified as Jews."

"How do you know all this information? You never mentioned it to me."

"I'd forgotten about that until now. It goes back to my student days when I spent a year in Warsaw. That winter I attended a series of lectures at night, sponsored by Hashomer Hatzair. One of the lectures was called: "Anti-Semitism through the Ages." Somewhere in one of the drawers I still have the notes with the exact dates of those anti-Semitic laws."

Lena had looked off, vacantly, into space, as though projecting herself into those various centuries Hershel had mentioned. Then she had sighed deeply and said, "It's small comfort to know that the yellow badge has such a long history."

He had arrived at the square without his armband. He had pulled it off the sleeve before he left the building where he worked. Though he knew what the consequences could be if he were caught he banked on his appearance, which was not particularly Jewish. Wearing his cap jauntily to the side and smoking a cigarette he could easily pass for a Pole. And he had the added advantage of speaking Polish without a trace of an accent.

There were times when he took the risk out of sheer defiance, or just for the pleasure of not being stared at and singled out in a crowd. But today he did it for practical reasons. The armband made the wearer a visible target to roving hoodlums who, when they saw a Jew enter a store, waited outside then forced him to give up what he'd bought. Well, he wasn't going to buy a crib only to have it taken away from him by some hoodlums.

The store was dimly lighted (the looters had carried off the floor lamps together with the furniture). Among

22

the few pieces on display Hershel did not see a crib. "Anything you see here, sir," the storekeeper said in Polish, "you can have at half price. I'm selling out."

Hershel was pleased that he was taken for a Pole, but the man looked anxious and tense so he set him at ease by introducing himself in Yiddish, "I am Hershel Bregman." Dantziger smiled and shook his hand warmly. "Please forgive me, Pan Bregman. You did look familiar when you entered but not seeing your armband I thought I was in error. Do you have some kind of special permission not to wear it?"

"There's no such thing for the armband. I gave myself permission."

"You're a brave man, Pan Bregman."

"My wife thinks I'm a foolish man."

"If, God forbid, you're caught she will be right. But I hear you're not the only one. I hear that some women, who don't look particularly Jewish and speak a good Polish, put on a cross and leave the armband at home when they go shopping for food. Yes," he added with a sigh, "who would have thought that five centuries after Torquemada we would have Marranos again."

"But we've outlived Torquemada and we'll outlive Hitler too. I'm an optimist, Pan Dantziger."

"You must be if you came to buy furniture. Jews are selling these days, not buying. What is it you want, Pan Bregman?"

"What I want I don't see," he said, surveying the store again. "I need a baby crib."

"I believe I have one down in the basement. These days the less you have on display the better." He went to the back of the store, descended a few steps and a minute later returned with a brown-colored crib. "Mahogany," he announced, "the finest."

"I'll take it," Hershel said, and paid the man at once.

As they shook hands Dantziger said, "Let me wish you *mazeltov*, Pan Bregman. And may the children of Israel continue to multiply despite the von Holtzers.

And may your wife have an easy delivery. When, if I may ask, is she expecting?"

"Not for some time yet. She's only in her second month."

"And you're already buying a crib. Apparently you don't place much stock in that ghetto rumor."

"On the contrary. I think that's where we'll end up."

"And still you're buying a crib?"

"Where will one get a crib in the ghetto? And at half price yet?"

"You're a man of foresight, Pan Bregman. Now tell me something. Since you do take the rumor seriously, where do you think the ghetto will be?"

"In the worst section of town, of course. Where else would von Holtzer put the Jews?"

"You mean where the second pump is?"

"That's right. Heat only from stoves. Water only from the pump. The toilet in the hallway. Hallways dark and foul-smelling. Rooms small and depressing. Rats, roaches, and bugs."

"A beautiful future you're planning for us, Pan Bregman. Though my heart tells me you're right, I hope you're wrong."

"I hope so, too, Pan Dantziger."

3

ON A FRIDAY NOON, about two weeks after Hershel had bought the crib, posters on walls announced, in both German and Polish, the transfer of the Jews from their homes to a ghetto. They had twenty-four hours to get ready. They were to appear the next day at noon on the square with their belongings. They could take with them whatever they could carry except furniture.

When Hershel read the poster the first question that occurred to him was whether Germans would regard the crib as furniture. It was a child's bed and, given the German mentality, they could be technical about it and put it in that category. Besides, it was brand new and mahogany. For this alone they might not let him keep it. For some reason it would pain him more to have to leave the crib behind than all the other pieces they had bought at Dantziger's three years ago when they were married.

His mind began to work at once on a plan to salvage it. He would somehow scrounge up an old baby carriage, remove the body, attach a wooden board over the wheels, attach the crib to the board, and thus turn the whole thing into a pushcart, filled with whatever belongings they could cram into it. He knew he could do it. The question was when. The Jews had twenty-four hours to get ready but they still had to be on their jobs today. That meant working through the night.

Around four in the afternoon the young architect Tadeusz Bielowski, an official in the Housing Department, appeared on the construction site to check on the progress of the work. He made such inspection visits at least three times a week. Hershel liked him because he treated all workers, both Jews and non-Jews, alike

Whereas the foreman, also a Pole, had one kind of treatment for Jews and another for Poles, Bielowski always addressed him as Pan Bregman and openly praised his work; the foreman had one name for every Jew, *zhidek*.

When Bielowski came over to Hershel he said in a low voice, "I'm sorry to hear you're moving tomorrow, Pan Bregman. By the way, do you have a water barrel at home?"

Hershel shook his head. "We get our water from a faucet."

"Well, if you can get your hand on one take it along. It might come in handy."

Hershel thanked him and, after hesitating a moment, said, "Pan Bielowski, may I ask you a favor?"

"Please."

"It's in connection with tomorrow's moving. Is it possible to get off a little earlier today so that I can have time to pack?"

"Let me talk to the foreman."

On the way out of the building the architect whispered to Hershel, "I told him I need you to fix a loose connection in my office and that you'll go home from there. Where do you live?" When Hershel told him the address he said, "That's on the way, I'll take you in the car and you'll save yourself a walk." He told the chauffeur where to let Hershel off and to Hershel he said, "On Monday you go back to the same place. If they take you elsewhere tell them my orders are for ʋu to go to the old job."

"Thank you, sir."

ʾo his surprise he found Lena home. The head nurse ʾet the Jewish women on the staff go home earlier

it were up to our foreman," Hershel said, "I'd ə working. I'm here thanks to that young architect, ʋski. He's a real decent Pole. By the way, we'll ɔ scrounge up a barrel someplace."

ıy a barrel?"

"That was his advice. He must know what he's talking about, otherwise he wouldn't have said it. Don't forget, from now on it's goodby faucet. We'll be back to pumping again."

"You know, I never thought about it, not once."

"So it's a good thing he reminded us."

"Where will you get a barrel?"

"I'll talk to the janitor. He has all kinds of junk in the cellar. If he doesn't have one, he'll get one. I'll grease his palm. That always works. I'll also need an old baby carriage."

"A baby carriage!" she stared at him with astonishment. "What for?"

"Not for the baby, for the crib."

"A baby carriage for the crib!" She burst out laughing. "Hershel stop talking in riddles to me."

"I know it sounds funny but we need an old baby carriage to save the new crib," and he explained the reason why. "I know I can do it," he said. "The main thing is finding one. And that assignment I'll also give to the janitor. I'll tell him I'll make it worth his while."

It turned out the janitor did have an old baby carriage in the cellar, but not a barrel. He promised to find one before curfew and succeeded.

They had been up most of the night packing and the most difficult thing for Lena was deciding what to take and what to leave behind. Every piece of possession, even things hidden away in drawers and in closets that hadn't been looked at in years suddenly assumed a new importance. "Take us," they seemed to plead. "Do not abandon us." They spoke with the voice of memories and sentiments, of special moods and special occasions. This was a birthday gift from Hershel; that a wedding present from a dear friend; this was bought on a holiday trip in Warsaw; that on their honeymoon in Zakopane. The Chanukah menorah, a family heirloom, was given them by her parents; the silver-plated candlesticks by his.

Drawers and closets were emptied, their contents heaped on the bed, the sofa, the table, the floor. A jumble of dissimilar things, a lifetime of proud order-liness turned into chaos.

Lena stood in the middle of the room, her eyes moving from heap to heap. What should she tackle first, the clothing? The dishes? The silverware? The bedding? The photographs collected over the years? The school diplomas? The books? What did one take to a ghetto? She asked herself. She knew she had to do *something,* that every minute counted, but she was so overwhelmed by the task she couldn't move. She burst into tears.

Hershel stopped working on the hand wagon and came into the living room. He put his arms around Lena. "I don't know where to begin," she said, sobbing. Neither did he. But he knew he must tell her something, something that would dispel the paralysis. "Begin with what is most necessary and most valuable," he suggested. "Of these we will take what we can carry. The rest we'll leave behind. Survival. That is our main concern now. At this moment only those things that'll help us survive are essential. The rest is unimportant."

Hershel was about to go back to work on the wagon when his eye caught the stack of books in a corner of the floor. He walked over and began picking titles and laying them aside.

"Don't run away with yourself, Hershel," she warned. "Where will you put them?"

"Just a few. You can always squeeze in a book here and a book there. How can you not take at least one Sholem Aleichem?"

"One. That's all we can take."

"All right, which one?"

"Any one is all right with me. Sholem Aleichem is Sholem Aleichem."

They settled for *Tevyeh the Dairyman.*

In addition to Sholem Aleichem he picked one by Peretz, one by Asch, and one by Bialik. "And what of the Polish poets?" he asked, "Tuwim, Slonimski, Mickiewicz?"

"I don't know what to say. I like them all."

28

"So let's take them. I'll find room for them."

When she saw him pull yet another volume from the heap she cried out, "Hershel!"

"I found them!" he exclaimed, triumphantly. "The lecture notes I've been looking for in all the drawers. Here they are. Stuck in a volume of Dubnov's *History of the Jews*." He sat down on the edge of a crowded chair and began to turn the yellowing, closely written notes. "Remember I told you about the ghettos in Rome? Here it is. The name of the pope was Paul IV, and the year was 1555. The Jews had to wear yellow hats and were allowed to trade only in second-hand clothing. And the blood libels which still crop up now and then, you know how far they go back? To 1247."

"Hershel, is this the time to dig up the old anti-Semitism when we're trying to cope with von Holtzer's brand new version?"

"That's what I'm trying to tell you. It's not new."

"The fact that Jews suffered in the past doesn't make my suffering now any easier. It only shows that *our* history repeats itself. Please finish what you have to do on the wagon. I need your help here."

He rose and put the notes back into the Dubnov volume. She watched him standing with his back to her near the little heap of books he'd selected to take along, deliberating. Then he quickly added the Dubnov volume. As he walked past her she looked at him, smiling knowingly.

"Don't worry," he assured her. "I'll find room for one more. For years I haven't touched Dubnov. Suddenly I have an urge to go back to Jewish history."

4

It was the last Saturday in November, almost three months to the day since the German tank had rumbled into town. It was cold but in a bracing way. The air had a sharp, prewinter bite to it and was transparently clear. The sky was a pale blue without even a hint of a cloud. It was a sunny, lovely day. A day for almost anything but marching into a ghetto.

In normal times Jews would now be coming home from the synagogue, wishing each other *gut shabbos*. Dressed in their holiday attire they would be walking home leisurely to a warm Sabbath meal and an afternoon nap. But on this Sabbath Jews were hurrying to the square, hurrying but making slow progress because after every few steps they had to pause and rest. They were loaded down with a lifetime of possessions reduced to whatever their hands and backs could carry. Bent under the weight of huge bundles wrapped in bedsheets, or small trunks hoisted on shoulders, their heads and faces were barely visible.

By noon the square was so densely packed with people and bundles it was difficult to turn around. And they were still coming. Like Lena and Hershel they had agonized to the very last minute what to take and what to leave behind. Now there was panic in their eyes. They were fearful of the consequences of being late. Even for one's imprisonment one had to be on time. The square was so crowded it seemed there was no room left for even one more straggler, but the push of a rifle butt or the mere threat of one somehow created space for yet another pair of feet. Now the square was packed to suffocation. If only the Germans would give the order to march, what a relief that would be.

They were still standing when a woman discovered that one of her children was missing, a little girl of five. "Peshele, Peshele," she kept wailing. "What will happen to my Peshele?"

"Nothing will happen to her," someone tried to assure her. "Somebody is probably holding her by the hand right now." But the woman would not be placated and tried to push her way out of the crowd. A German soldier materialized. *"Was ist los?"* he barked.

"Mein Kind, mein Kind," the woman wailed.

"Stehn bleiben!" he aimed his rifle at her, his finger on the trigger. The woman screamed. The others fell back in horror. An eternity seemed to have passed before the German removed his finger from the trigger and slung the rifle back on his shoulder.

The woman lost the sympathy of those around her. "Look what you've done with your foolishness," they shouted at her. "You could have gotten killed and others with you."

"You call losing a child foolish?"

"You haven't lost her. She's there, somewhere in the crowd. But you've come close to making her an orphan."

The woman slumped down on her bundle. "My child, my Peshele," she whimpered. Her other children, two boys and a girl, clung to her, crying, "Mama, Mama." Someone in the back was heard saying, "I know her. She's a widow." Sympathy for the woman was rekindled. People talked to her in soft, consoling tones: "Your child is safe, believe me. As soon as we begin to move it'll be easier to look for her."

"You think so?" the woman looked up at her consoler.

"Of course. It's common sense."

A shot rang out, piercing the air with its incisive report. The shot was followed by a commotion somewhere in the back of the line. The Poles on the side-lines, now grown into a huge crowd, suddenly turned into a human tidal wave rushing in the direction of the gunshot. The Jews, hemmed in by each other and their fear of the guards, remained fixed in their places. Those who managed to turn and crane their heads could see little. Their vision was blocked by the bundles of the Jews behind them and the crowd of onlookers.

The mother of the missing child leaped to her feet. "My Peshele! My Peshele!" she cried. "Something has happened to my Peshele." Once again she attempted to break out of the line, but was restrained by the others. "Are you out of your mind?" they shouted at her from all sides. "The first time you were lucky. The next time he'll shoot you. You're a danger to all of us." They took her by her arms and forcibly lowered her down on her bundle.

A sketchy account of the shooting incident was rapidly passed down the line by word of mouth. By the time it reached Lena and Hershel, who were somewhere near the middle of the line, this is what was pieced together: Mordecai Dantziger, the furniture dealer, was shot. It seemed he'd hired a drayman to transport his belongings. This in itself was not illegal. But since he was the only one to enjoy such comfort, he made himself conspicuous and aroused the Germans' curiosity. They poked around and found, under a heap of clothing, a brand new chair from his own store. This *was* illegal. The posters said it was forbidden to take furniture.

Dantziger was punished on the spot. First he was ordered to dump his belonging onto the ground. Then he was told to stand next to the object of his crime— the chair. When the German lieutenant in charge was satisfied with the pose he drew his pistol from the holster and shot him point blank. He then pulled two Jews from the line and ordered them to put Dantziger's corpse on the wagon. As soon as the officer had walked away from the scene some of the onlookers on the sidelines made a rush for the scattered belongings and in no time they were gone. Two young Poles fought over the chair until it broke. Frustrated, they began beating each other with the pieces left in their hands until a German soldier pulled them apart.

After hearing the story a Jew standing next to Hershel commented: "So now we're in a funeral procession. Except that the corpse is in the back instead of the front." To which another Jew retorted: "And where were we before Dantziger was shot, not in a funeral procession?"

When the water carrier's widow found herself in full view of the pump, and only a few steps from where her husband had been shot, she let out a moan and fainted. There was nowhere for her to fall. The very crowdedness kept her on her feet. Still, her two sons held her by her arms to prevent her from falling. "Mama, Mama," they whimpered in the voice of small children. "Slap her face," someone in the crowd suggested to one of the sons; but he couldn't bring himself to do it, so a stranger did it and brought her to. People pushed back as far as possible so that she could lean against Hershel's wagon.

At last the line began to move. Because everyone was loaded down with baggage it got off to a slow, uneven start. Bundles were lifted, hoisted on shoulders, adjusted and readjusted. There were no empty hands, no empty backs. The quick and efficient impatiently pushed their way past the slow and the helpless and moved ahead. The number of those falling behind was growing. The Germans would have none of that. Soldiers ran up and down the line barking, *"Schneller! Schneller!"* their rubber truncheons and rifle butts setting a fast pace.

The woman who had been waiting for the line to move so that she could run back and look for her lost child now found that it couldn't be done. Every time she attempted to step out of her row she was swept forward by a fast-moving human tide. She muttered accusations at those on either side of her. "I shouldn't have listened to them," she said, bitterly, as though to herself. "I should have looked for my child when there was still time." No one paid any attention to

33

her. Everyone concentrated on keeping up with the pace of those in front of them; on dodging the rubber truncheons.

Suddenly someone up ahead was slowing down the march. It was the rabbi, an ailing man in his sixties. He was carrying a Torah scroll, wrapped in a pillow case, the only Torah scroll the Jews were able to save. (The other three were desecrated by the Germans during the Yom Kippur pogrom.) Several Jews had volunteered to carry the rabbi's belongings so that his hands would be free for the Torah. But the pace was too fast for him. He was growing weak, falling behind.

"Will someone take the Torah from me before it falls from my hands?" the rabbi pleaded.

There were no free hands. Bundles had to be set down, shifted and reshifted in a quick and intricate exchange until a hand was freed. But the rabbi was too weak to go on even without the Torah. His face was pale and he was breathing with difficulty. A soldier came running up the line. *"Donnerwetter!"* he shouted, brandishing his truncheon.

"Go. Go on without me," the rabbi urged the others. "You'll endanger your lives."

"Marsch!" the soldier barked, holding the truncheon over the rabbi's head.

At that moment, Yoshke the porter, a giant of a Jew, appeared as if from nowhere, dropped his own load, grabbed the rabbi's arms and hoisted him on his back. The line moved on. "But . . . your things . . . your possessions . . ." the rabbi protested.

"They aren't worth carrying, Rabbi," Yoshke replied.

Miraculously, hands fully occupied and strained to the uttermost found the strength to grip yet another bundle, and Yoshke's things were not left behind.

The crowd of onlookers stretched along the whole line of the march. Some stared in silent fascination, as though they were watching a parade staged for their amusement. Some, particularly the young, jeered and laughed and made mocking gestures, imitating Jews

34

praying or twirling their earlocks. Here and there an elderly woman shook her head sadly and brushed a tear from her eyes. Here and there a hand went up, waving to a familiar face in the marching line. A former neighbor, or a friend perhaps.

Several young hoodlums ran in the middle of the street, parallel with the march, "Your day has come, Jews!" "Take a good look at the town, Jews. It's the last time you're seeing it."

"Shame, shame," an onlooker's feeble voice pursued them. But they paid no attention. It was the old woman who had crossed herself over the water carrier's corpse. She was still in black. A permanent mourner, it seemed.

An old Jew could not go on. His legs would not take him one more step. His wife stood near him, wringing her hands. The marchers swerved around them and passed them. A Polish policeman appeared on the scene. "Have pity on us," the woman pleaded. "He's a sick man. His heart. . . ." she said, and quickly pushed something into the policeman's hand. He looked to either side. The German soldiers were busy elsewhere. Just then the wagon with Dantziger's corpse was riding by. The policeman ordered the driver to halt and pick up the old couple with their belongings. Then he quickly disappeared. "What luck!" one of the marchers said, following the wagon with envious eyes.

5

THE TOWN'S two thousand Jews had to fit themselves into the space of two and a half streets henceforth known as the ghetto. The Germans' official name for it was *Judisches Wohnbezirk*—Jewish Quarter—but nobody, including the Germans, paid any attention to that euphemism.

All day that Saturday, and late into the night, the *Judenrat* had been busy allocating living space to the ghetto Jews, assigning as many as six, eight, and even ten people to a single room. Violent fights had broken out among the occupants over who had prior claim to the corner space, or the space near the window, and the Jewish police had to be called on to settle the disputes. By midnight there were still people sitting on their bundles in the street, waiting for a place to lay their heads down.

More than once that day Hershel remembered the architect, Bielowski, with gratitude for having suggested that he take along a barrel. Who, in those frantic twenty-four hours the Jews were given to get ready for the ghetto, had the presence of mind to think about water barrels? The handful that had was now looked upon with envy by the rest of the ghetto. For as soon as people had found their little space for themselves and their bundles, and the women had begun to think about boiling up some water for a glass of tea they realized that the water barrels were missing. The former tenants had taken them with them. They had to line up at the pump with their pots and pans and tea kettles.

As a result a brisk business had sprung up around the pump. As soon as the word was out that there was a barrel shortage in the ghetto Poles came from far and near with barrels of all sizes and sold them at prices double and triple their worth. That was in the days when the ghetto was still open; that is, Jews were not allowed out but Poles were allowed in at certain hours of the day to barter and sell. In exchange for clothing articles and bedsheets the Jews obtained some bread, dairy products, and vegetables. Thus they supplemented the ghetto starvation rations.

So the barrel problem was solved and the food shortage was somewhat eased. But the problem to which there seemed to be no solution was the crowdedness. Total strangers were thrown together in the most intimate settings. The floor became a communal bed. Occupants became known by the smell of their bodies, the sound of their snores. To open a window meant to freeze; to keep it closed meant to suffocate. Infants wailed. Men fought over an inch of space. Women quarreled over the use of the stove. To get into the hallway toilet was a major achievement. People would have gladly parted with a most precious possession for a little privacy.

And there was nowhere to escape. One went from a crowded room to a crowded street. To get from one end of the street to another one had to brave a continuous stream of people going in the opposite direction. One's arms and shoulders hurt from the jostling and bumping; one's feet grew tired from dodging the steps of others' feet. Still it was better than being inside. But one had that choice only until the curfew hour. After eight o'clock one *had* to be inside.

With it all life in the ghetto squirmed and squeezed itself into a pattern of existence that, on the surface at least, took on the appearance of normalcy, which led many to believe that the worst was over. What the Germans wanted they already had, these Jews reasoned. They wanted our homes, our possessions, our businesses, and they have them. They got us out of their way and they still have our forced labor. From now on they'll probably leave us alone. They'll probably even forget about the rumored barbed wire fence that was to go up any day.

One morning, on a day of the fifth week, a crew of Polish workers arrived with several huge rolls of barbed wire and began to enclose the ghetto under the supervision of a German overseer. The work took four days. When it was completed the *Judenrat* was presented with an itemized bill. So much for the wire; so much for labor; so much for feeding the workers while on the job.

Suddenly the two and a half streets had shrunk to the size of a large prison cell. As long as the streets were open and the barrier that stood between them and the rest of the population consisted of a decree and several guards the Jews had the illusion of still being part of the town. The barbed wire fence put an end to that illusion and made their isolation from the rest of the world complete.

And they were isolated even from the pump that stood only a few feet away from the ghetto. Because of the three houses still inhabited by Polish families who, for some reason had not been relocated with the others, von Holtzer had decreed that the pump remain outside the ghetto for their convenience. Poles should not have to demean themselves by going into the ghetto for their water. It had to be demonstrated to the Polish population that the lowliest Poles were held in higher esteem than the Jews.

That was not all. Poles, the decree stated, could come to the pump whenever they wished, but the ghetto Jews could draw water only between six and eight in the morning. A small gate was constructed for just that purpose—to let the Jews out with their empty barrels and let them return with their full ones. The gate was guarded by a German soldier and a Jewish policeman.

With the erection of the barbed wire fence came yet another decree that hit the ghetto hardest of all: Henceforth Aryans will not be allowed in the ghetto.

An end to the bartering of old clothes for food! An end to the supplementing of starvation rations!

Still some Jews found a way. Despite the fact that smuggling food into the ghetto was strictly forbidden, and in some cases even punishable by death, a new type of Jew arose in the ghetto—the smuggler. Life in the ghetto had to be lived one day at a time, and all of one's energy, wits, and ingenuity had to be harnessed to that purpose. It was a full-time occupation.

6

THE GHETTO HOSPITAL was a makeshift affair, a converted warehouse once used for sorting flour and grain. During the Yom Kippur looting the heavily bolted door had been battered down and the place broken into. Youngsters and women who couldn't lift the one-hundred-pound sacks slit them open and spilled part of the contents on the floor. This attracted the neighborhood rats. The door, which was left hanging on one hinge, was always ajar and this was an invitation to stray dogs. Passersby walked in to relieve themselves. In a matter of three months the warehouse had become an outhouse.

When Dr. Weiss heard that this was to be the hospital he was appalled. "This pigsty?!" he exclaimed. "The stench of urine and feces is so strong you can't cross the threshold. Besides, it has no electricity, no plumbing, and it has a cement floor."

"There are no other buildings available," the head of the *Judenrat* told him. "It's this or nothing. Plumbing is out of the question. Electricity, maybe. The cement floors can be covered with wooden boards. But first it must be cleaned out, and for that I'll give you all the labor you need."

About a dozen workers were assigned to the job. They scrubbed the floor, washed the walls, removed the iron grates from the windows to admit a little more sunlight, put the door back on its hinges, repaired the lock, installed an old potbelly stove in the center of the room. But there were no boards to cover the floor. Because coal was practically nonexistent wood had become a scarce commodity in the ghetto. By the first

40

week of January people were already using their furniture for firewood to cook a meal or to keep from freezing. So the cement floor became a crazy quilt of old newspapers, pieces of thick burlap, and rags.

After all this had been done the warehouse was disinfected with carbolic acid. When the head of the *Judenrat* came by to inspect it he turned to Dr. Weiss and said, "What did I tell you? It already smells like a hospital."

"That it does," the doctor replied. "Now we need a hospital."

"Give me a list of what you need and I'll see what I can do."

"The list is a very simple one. I will need a fluoroscope, an X-ray machine, some surgical instruments, some drugs and vaccines, a supply of cotton and gauze, and some soap. . . ."

The *Judenrat* man nodded, smiling ironically. "That's an impossible list, doctor," he finally said, seriously. "I cannot deliver a single item on it. All I can do is submit it to von Holtzer's office, and I know in advance what the answer will be—no."

"You asked for a list, I gave you a list."

"I meant a realistic one. Let me tell you what I can do. I can scrounge up some beds for you. I know I can get some old army cots. As for bedding, I can't promise you anything. They've bartered away for food most of what they could spare. The patients may have to bring their own bedding. When we get a supply of coal, the hospital will get priority. The same goes for wood."

"You haven't said anything about food. The minimum requirement is three thousand calories per person per day and all the Germans allow us is not quite three hundred. For the hospital at least the rations should be five times that much."

"Now you're again asking for the impossible. Still, in this area we may be able to do something. Just between us," he lowered his voice confidentially, "if we juggle the figures a little . . . raise the number of patients now and then . . . the rations will be increased. . . ."

"So when all is said and done," the doctor nodded disconsolately, "I'm still ending up with a smell of carbolic acid and not with a hospital."

The *Judenrat* man made no reply. But when he was about to leave, he said, "As for that medical list . . . all may not be lost there either. For a heavy bribe maybe we can wrangle something from them. The Germans like 'gifts' . . . gold . . . jewelry . . . we'll see what we can do."

"How about staff?"

"People I'll give you all you want."

"I want my former nurse, Lena Bregman, as my head nurse."

"As I said, anyone you want. And give me in writing that medical list you mentioned."

One week later the doctor was called to the *Judenrat* office. The *Judenrat* head, a spry-looking man in his late forties, leaned back in his chair, smiling triumphantly. "I have a surprise for you, doctor," he said, pointing to a small carton on his desk. "You know what's in there?"

"I know," the doctor nodded. "Instruments."

"That's right. At first the answer was no to everything. But I didn't come empty-handed and their medical officer, a Captain Stehlmann, is no different from the rest of them when it comes to gifts. A gold watch for him and a gold bracelet for Frau Stehlmann softened him a little. At least enough to let us have the instruments."

Dr. Weiss took the instruments out of the carton and laid them out on the desk. "They go back to the days of the clinic," he explained. "When we opened the new hospital, it was new in every respect, including the latest and most up-to-date instruments. I retired these to the stockroom, in this very same carton, and hoped that some day I'd have them thoroughly polished and placed in a showcase in my office as a memento of bygone days and as a symbol of the progress we'd made. Some progress!" he said, bitterly, after a long pause. *"Our* hospital. We built it with *our* sweat and *our* money. And when it was finished, we opened its doors to Jew and Gentile alike . . . and now we have to go begging for a piece of cotton and a piece of gauze, a few instruments. And speaking of cotton and gauze, I should tell you that so far I have been managing with what I took along from my own office. I have enough to last me for just another few days. Maybe for another gold watch . . ."

"I tried, doctor. Nothing doing. Not even some soap."

"So he parted only with what was totally useless to them—the old instruments. Then you will have to supply the cotton and gauze."

"I?" the *Judenrat* man looked at him with surprise.

"Yes. This is something, I'm sure, you *can* do. I will need some old bedsheets. They could be torn and useless. And I will need a cotton mattress, even if it's full of holes. Try to get me these items at once."

"Torn sheets and a cotton mattress?" the *Judenrat* head now looked perplexed.

"The cotton from the mattress will be boiled and sterilized. That will give us cotton. We'll do the same with the sheets and that will give us bandages."

"Doctor, I can see we'll have a hospital."

"And, of course, we already have the smell," the doctor added, smiling ironically.

7

THE ONE BRIGHT SPOT in Lena's and Hershel's ghetto life was their newly won privacy. Thanks to Dr. Weiss's concern for Lena's state of pregnancy, and to Hershel's "golden hands," they now had a room in the hospital all to themselves. Dr. Weiss, a fifty-five year old widower, whose only son, a lawyer, had been killed in the defense of Warsaw in September 1939, was the only other occupant of a single room. The rest of the staff, including the young Dr. Margolis, lived outside the hospital.

Their room had to be created, "carved out," as Hershel put it, in the sprawling structure of the warehouse. He grafted on a wooden wall and a door; constructed a table and two benches; found a small stove with a single burner and pieced together enough pipe to feed the smoke into the main chimney. The bed was one of a motley of beds the *Judenrat* had gathered for the hospital. Hershel had done all the work on the room in the evenings, after his day's work on the forced labor job. (That was in the days before the barbed wire when returning laborers were still allowed to bring into the ghetto bundles of firewood or pieces of board for construction.)

Finally there was the closet. It had come with a heap of old furniture the *Judenrat* had rounded up for the hospital. Dr. Weiss had no use for it and rather than send it back offered it to Lena. Hershel then went to work on it and converted it into a catchall for all of their possessions. He built shelves on either side of it, which took the place of a chest of drawers. He fashioned clothes hangers from castaway pieces of wire and supplemented those with all kinds of hooks and nails. He improvised a "bookcase," a "shoe rack," and a secret "vault" for their few pieces of jewelry and important documents such as birth certificates and school diplomas. They had been living out of the crib. Now they were able to move most of the things into the closet.

Very quickly life was forced into a set routine. Their alarm clock would go off at 5:30 in the morning. An hour later Hershel would report at the main gate and be marched off, with his forced labor brigade, to his work project outside the ghetto. Most of that hour was taken up with waiting in line in front of the privy. Even those not attached to a labor brigade rose at dawn. Survival demanded that the ghetto be on its feet at sunup.

The eight o'clock curfew drove the people off the streets and turned the ghetto into a prison within a prison. Nowhere to go, and exhausted from the long day's struggle for existence, they went to bed. One evening Hershel rebelled. "I'm not going to let von Holtzer turn me into a work robot," he said to Lena. "Work, work, work, from dawn to dusk, a bite of food and to bed so the body can rest up for the next round of work, work, work. That's how it must have been when the Jews were slaves in Egypt under Pharaoh. Even a horse is allowed to roam the field a little before it is returned to the stable."

"And where will you roam, my dear horse, when the whole field consists of two-and-a half muddy streets and even they are closed to you during curfew?"

"If I can't roam, my soul can. Von Holtzer's curfews do not apply to my soul." He walked over to the closet and pulled out the Dubnov volume they had taken along. "I will let my soul loose in the fields of our people's history. My soul has been starving. It needs a little nourishment. We are fortunate in that we have a room to ourselves. We have the privacy to read a book, even aloud to each other, and we're not taking advantage of it. From now on, just as an orthodox Jew begins his day by donning his phylacteries I will end my day with a little Dubnov, or a little Peretz, or a little Sholem Aleichem. You can go to bed if you feel like it. I am going to read awhile."

"My soul also needs some nourishment," she said, and sat down on the bench next to him. For the next hour they read aloud to each other. From that time on reading together became a nightly ritual they looked forward to. It gave them a sense of continuity with their former life which already seemed to have receded into the distant past.

Lena sat at the table, trying to knit a cotton baby sacque by the light of the kerosene lamp. Every now and then she had to stop and rub her fingers together, or exhale her warm breath on them to keep them from growing stiff. The room had not been heated for several days and the accumulated cold, plus the dampness exuding from the stone walls and cement floor, penetrated the several layers of clothing she had on beneath her winter coat and made her bones ache.

Earlier Hershel had been reading aloud but had had to stop because of the cold. Now he was pacing the floor back and forth to quicken his circulation and stop shivering. Lena was both too tired and too heavy for pacing. She was in the sixth month of her pregnancy and had been on her feet all day at the ward. She glanced at the small alarm clock that stood near the lamp. "Hershel, you know what time it is?" He seemed not to have heard her. "It's half-past nine." When again he made no reply she looked up from her knitting. He was staring into the doorless closet, as though transfixed. A week ago, one night, he had removed the closet door from its hinges and hacked it to pieces. "We can do without the closet," he'd said, justifying his deed. "You're in the hospital all day so there's no danger of someone stealing anything." She'd said nothing. Others in the ghetto had already gone beyond using furniture for firewood. In desperation some were pulling boards from walls and rafters from ceilings.

"Hershel, are you going to burn the shelves too? All that work you put in. It's a shame."

He walked away from the closet and began to pace the floor again. Suddenly it grew quiet in the room. His pacing had come to a halt. She looked up and saw him standing in front of the crib, staring at it with the same transfixed look he had a while ago when he was standing in front of the closet. He was unaware that she was watching him with a near-hysterical cry, "No, Hershel! No! Not the crib!"

He was so startled by her cry and the pained expression on her face he began to shake. For a moment he seemed glued to the floor, as though too stunned to move. Then he walked over to the table and sat down on the bench next to her. "I couldn't have done it," he said, sounding contrite. "I know I couldn't have done it. But the mere fact that I even thought of doing it makes me feel ashamed. Forgive me?"

"Of course I forgive you. But you must promise me that no matter how cold it gets you'll not be tempted to chop up the crib. Promise?"

"I promise," he said, taking her around.

"Now let's go to bed." And to give him courage to undress in the cold she began to remove her coat.

Just then there was a light knock on the door. Hershel went to see who it was. It was Dr. Weiss. "Forgive me," he said, "But I saw the light was on . . ."

They knew that something extraordinary must have happened. Dr. Weiss rarely knocked at that hour, light or no light. When there was an emergency on the ward it was usually the nurse on duty or the male orderly that knocked. Hershel pulled out a bench for the doctor and Lena put her coat on again.

"I've just been to the *Judenrat*," the doctor announced. "They sent for me to tell me about von Holtzer's latest . . . something that concerns you too, that's why I felt I should talk to you tonight." He paused, lowering his head as though unable to face them with the news. "Tomorrow . . ." he began and paused again, "Tomorrow it will be posted on the walls. . . . Henceforth, pregnancies will be forbidden

47

in the ghetto." He'd said it, and now he looked straight at them. They sat in stunned silence, looking back at him in disbelief. Finally Hershel said, "Henceforth. But what about those that are already pregnant?"

"That's just it," the doctor, said, nodding. "The decree does not specify. The Germans who have a penchant for spelling out their decrees in great detail are suddenly very vague. Frankly, I'm suspicious about this vagueness. So much so that when one of the *Judenrat* people suggested that they ask for clarification I advised against it. You know the saying: 'If you ask a question, you get an answer.' And the answer, in this instance, could be the kind we don't want. Supposing they say that the decree applied to future pregnancies only, and at the same time they ask for a list of those already pregnant. Do I have to tell you what the Germans do with such lists? One day they can show up with the list in their hands and round them all up for deportation."

Lena, who had been too shocked to speak, now broke her silence: "So you think women in my condition should do nothing?"

"Quite the contrary," the doctor replied, "It's about women in your condition that I am most concerned. Those who are still in the early stage of their pregnancy I will urge to have an abortion. But you are too far gone for that."

"What am I to do?" she asked in despair.

"Women who must go through with their pregnancies will have to keep out of von Holtzer's sight. Of any German's sight. They will have to have their deliveries in secret; and they'll have to keep their infants a secret. How one can keep an infant a secret under these crowded conditions I don't know. In this respect, at least, you are fortunate. You have a room all to yourselves. The delivery can take place right here and you can keep your child a secret. The question is how to keep you a secret until the delivery."

"I can't see myself hiding in this room for three

months," Lena said. "I'll go out of my mind. I'll freeze to death."

"And I can't afford not having you on the ward. You're my head nurse. With frequent periods of rest you can work for another two months. The important thing is you shouldn't be around when von Holtzer or Dr. Stehlmann make one of their surprise visits. That's the time you should be in your room."

"But how can you guard against a surprise visit?" Hershel wanted to know.

"That's a problem. But I think it can be solved. They usually stop at the *Judenrat* first. I can talk to Gewirtzer and ask him to warn me in advance that they're coming over. I don't have to tell him the real reason. I can tell him I need a little time to tidy up the place. In addition, we should all be on the alert. Watchful. And speaking about being on the alert I would suggest that you get rid of this at once," he said, pointing to the crib.

"But that's for the baby," Lena exclaimed with alarm.

"That's precisely why you must dispose of it," the doctor said. "There's only one reason for the presence of a crib in a room—a baby."

"I'm sorry," Lena said, holding back her tears. "It was stupid of me not to see it."

"Not stupid, Lena, human. You're an expectant mother." He rose. "I'll let you two go to bed. Sorry to have been the messenger of bad news."

"Don't go yet, doctor," Hershel said, "Stay a while. We'll have some tea."

"Tea?" The doctor looked at the dead stove and at Hershel. "I know you have talented hands, but I didn't know you could perform miracles."

"Not miracles, doctor, merely taking your advice." He emptied the crib of a few household things it contained, took the hatchet from his tool box and, with several swift strokes, took it apart. Lena covered her eyes with her hands, sobbing softly. The doctor put his hand on her shoulder. "He's doing what he *has* to do, Lena," he said, consolingly. "You know he can

49

do wonders with his hands. Today he takes a crib apart. When the baby comes he may put one together. There's no telling what can happen three months from now."

Minutes later they were standing around the little stove, holding their hands over it as though in blessing for the warmth it gave them. When the water came to a boil Lena brewed some of the ersatz tea Hershel had smuggled in in his tool box one day. Their hands wrapped around the steaming glasses as they sipped the hot liquid with zest and relish. "Tea on a night like tonight," said the doctor, "tastes better than cognac."

"Not just tea," Hershel commented, "but tea cooked on a fire from the best mahogany wood!"

"Where else can a Jew have such luxuries if not in a ghetto?"

For the first time that evening Lena allowed herself a smile.

PART TWO

8

AT THE AGE OF ONE-AND-A-HALF little David was still a well-kept secret in the ghetto. Besides his parents and grandparents only the hospital staff knew of his existence. Because he could not be registered with the *Judenrat* his parents had to forego the claim to another ration card. But Dr. Weiss saw to it that the infant did not starve. He added one more patient to his daily list and thus boosted the hospital rations.

And, of course, there was his father. Now that he had an infant son to feed Hershel took greater risks pitting his wits against the brutality of the guards, smuggling some food into the ghetto. His skilled worker's certificate enabled him to take his tool box with him even when he worked on ordinary labor jobs that did not require the use of his special skills. He had equipped the box with various secret compartments large enough to hold a few ounces of butter or a few slices of lard. Once, when little David had contracted pneumonia and was hovering between life and death Hershel succeeded, for the price of a gold ring, in obtaining the necessary medicine and smuggling it into the ghetto.

The greatest challenge to his ingenuity came one day when he had the chance to buy a fresh egg. He had to decline the offer. His tool box was not equipped with a single secret compartment suitable for smuggling in something as fragile as an egg. "Sorry, babushka," he had to tell the woman, "I'm short in cash today. Some other time I'll be better prepared."

The thought of having to let an egg slip through his hands had bothered him for the rest of that day. His son had yet to taste an egg. That night he did not go to bed until he'd finished fashioning a round-shaped, hollow "tool" from a piece of sheet copper. He'd made it large enough to hold not one egg but two. He then soldered on a tube from the same copper for no other reason than to give it the authentic look of a tool. The next morning he began taking it with him to work so that the guards would get used to seeing it when they searched the tool box.

Eager to test the new gadget he began trying it out on foods that did not fit into the flat compartments— a potato, a beet, an onion, an apple. He took them all safely past the gate.

One day he had the opportunity to buy a herring. A commonplace item before the war but a real delicacy now in the ghetto. He couldn't resist the temptation. By rolling the herring tightly into a ball he was able to squeeze it into the copper receptacle. It was not until he'd opened the tool box for inspection that he realized his mistake. He hadn't counted on the smell. The herring had been in there since lunchtime and in the ensuing hours had filled the box with its distinctive aroma. The guard sniffed, crinkled his nose, then dumped the tools on the ground. It was a tense and anxious moment for Hershel as he watched the guard separate the tools with the toe of his boot. "All right. Pick 'em up!" he finally barked. Then he gave Hershel a thorough going over, passing his hands up and down his trousers, his sleeves, and turning his pockets inside out. Finally, still looking baffled, he let him go.

It was not until he was well within the ghetto grounds that he realized how perilously close he had been to catastrophe. Though he was no one to be easily frightened he was shaking inwardly from the experience. He decided not to tell Lena about it. When she asked, as always, "How did it go at the gate?" He replied, "Give me a plate and you'll see."

"You bought an egg!"

"No, not an egg. Do you still have some onion left?"

"I have half an onion."

"A half will do."

She placed the onion next to the plate and waited. Hershel opened the tool box and she looked in. "Am I supposed to see something here?" she asked.

"You're supposed to smell something. Put your nose in."

She lowered her head and sniffed inside the box. "Smells like herring," she said.

"You have a good nose." He pulled apart the copper "tool" and she gazed with amazement at the tightly curled fish. "It *is* a herring!" she exclaimed. "I'm surprised the guard didn't smell it."

"He probably has a cold."

"Hershel," she looked at him, shaking her head rebukingly. "What if he didn't have a cold, is it worth risking your life for a herring?"

"No. And I won't be tempted to do it again. But I'm here, and the herring is here, so let's celebrate."

From habit she was about to skin the herring before slicing it but changed her mind. Skinning a herring was a peacetime extravagance. Now it would be a criminal waste. She gave it a quick rinse to get the scales off without washing away any of the herring's natural juices. Then she sliced it carefully and evenly and trimmed it with onion rings. They both looked at it as though they were beholding a miracle. "Hershel," she said, "what do you think we call in Dr. Weiss and offer him some."

"I was thinking the same thing but hesitated to mention it."

"So I mentioned it. Go. And don't tell him anything. Just invite him in."

As soon as Hershel left the room she covered the plate with one of the linen napkins she'd brought along.

"Who will do the unveiling?" Hershel said, as the three of them stood around the table.

"That honor should go to the lady of the house," the doctor said, gesturing gallantly to Lena."

"I yield to you, doctor."

"Well, if you insist." He lifted the plate gingerly then stood back in astonishment. "My God, Hershel," he exclaimed. "I know you have talented hands but how did you sneak a herring past the guards?"

"Shall I reveal the secret, Lena?" Hershel said, with an impish wink.

"Yes," she nodded. "I think it's safe."

Hershel took his new "tool" from the box and handed it to the doctor.

"How the devil did you squeeze a herring through that narrow tube?" the doctor asked. "True, you have talented hands but you're not a magician."

With a quick twist of the hands Hershel took the "tool" apart.

"You *are* a magician," the doctor said, carefully examining the two halves of the receptacle.

"Actually, this was meant for smuggling in an egg, whenever I could get one. In the meantime a herring came along. How could I pass it up?"

The doctor was lost in thought. He was still studying the two halves of the "tool." Finally he said, "Hershel, you don't know how happy I am with your new invention. Only recently I succeeded in making contact with a pharmacist's clerk. Someone I know from the good old days. He promised me—for a tidy sum, of course—to give me some antityphus vaccine whenever he could get hold of it. These days this vaccine is worth its weight in gold. The problem was how to get it past the gate. If he brought it to you to your job would you be willing . . . ?"

"Do you have to ask, doctor?"

9

ONE APRIL DAY the forced labor brigades returned from their jobs to find their families crowding around the gate, pressing against the entire width of the barbed wire wall. Wives waved frantically to husbands and mothers to sons, their sad, tearstained faces lighting up in a momentary flicker of joy at the recognition of their dear ones. They had feared that what had happened in the ghetto had also happened on the jobs. They had not expected to see their men again.

As soon as the men had crossed the gate and heard the news a wail went up in the ghetto. The Germans had carried out an "action." Four-hundred Jews were dragged off to some unknown destination, mostly women, children, and the elderly. The nonproductive element, the Germans said.

There was hardly a family that was not touched by the "action." Hershel lost his mother and Lena both her parents. Miraculously little David was saved. Several SS men had barged into the hospital, their guns drawn. One of them grabbed Isaac and started pulling him out. "He's working here," Dr. Weiss had protested. "He's an orderly."

"You can do without one," the SS man retorted. "From now on there'll be less work here."

Another SS man kicked open the door to Lena's room, found it empty, and left with the others. Had he looked under the bed he would have discovered little David lying in a laundry basket that served as his crib, lying quietly, as though he knew that his very life depended on his silence.

* * *

That night the ghetto did not sleep. Remnants of families huddled together in despair and hope. The despair was deep and devastating, the hope illusory. The Germans had told the *Judenrat,* and the *Judenrat* had passed it on to the ghetto, that those taken in the "action" would be transported for "resettlement in the east," closer to the front, where they would be working for the German army and survive the war.

They spent hours agonizing over this story, trying to make it credible to themselves, giving it the kind of interpretation that would keep alive a hope: Who knows, maybe this time the Germans mean it. Closer to the front where there's a manpower shortage there may be work even for the elderly and the women— mending and washing uniforms, peeling potatoes. Who knows? But on the other hand, who can believe German promises? And what kind of work can they expect from four- and five-year-olds, from the sick and the infirm? They could hardly endure the journey to the front, let alone work there. But on the other hand. . . . They wanted desperately to cling to the slenderest of hopes, even if it was achieved by the most precious of reasonings.

And in the hospital, that night, in a room on whose door a wooden tablet said: ACHTUNG! TYPHUS! sat four men and a woman on the two empty cots. They were: Dr. Weiss, Hershel and Lena, Mendel— the water carrier's older son, Feivel, and Shymek, whom the underground had ordered to join the Jewish ghetto police so that it would be better informed about the doings of the *Judenrat*. It was Shymek who used to tip off Lena during her pregnancy and later when David was born whenever von Holtzer appeared in the ghetto.

These five, who constituted the leadership of some sixty-odd underground members, mostly young people of various political leanings, usually met in this room because it was the safest. The Germans would not get near this room because of their fear of the disease.

Even during an inspection Dr. Stehlmann would by-pass it, and only once in a great while he would make Dr. Weiss open the door because he would not touch the doorknob with his own hands.

Dr. Weiss kept the typhus patients in another part of the hospital, in the open ward, under a different diagnosis while the typhus room remained constantly empty so that he could tell the Germans that there were no typhus cases in the ghetto. In due time it became the underground's meeting place and for a while it was the hiding place of the only revolver the underground was able to obtain. The revolver was kept under the mattress of one of the cots. Now the only "weapons" concealed under the mattresses were two bottles of gasoline and several homemade hatchets. And what became of the revolver?

Three months earlier, on a cold February night, Feivel related the story of the revolver to his underground comrades in this very typhus room. It was a report of an ill-fated mission. His assignment had been to get himself to the forest, about twenty kilometers from town, and there try to make contact with the partisan detachment of the Home Army, which was operating somewhere in the region. He was to have told them that there were some young, combat-eager Jews in the ghetto ready to join the partisans and that he was sent to find out which was the quickest and safest way to get to the forest.

He had been on the same work brigade with Hershel then and the two had arranged that at a certain time during the brief lunch break Hershel would distract the guard's attention and at that moment Feivel would disappear. He would then pull the Star of David armband off his sleeve, head for the bus station and take the first bus out to the village nearest the forest. He had enough money to induce a peasant to provide him with a night's lodging, some food and, with a bit of luck, some information about the whereabouts of the partisans. He had a revolver to shoot his way out of a tight spot if it came to that. And he had a vial of cian-

58

kali, a poison that takes instant effect, in case he fell into the hands of the Germans.

Luck had been with him until the afternoon of the second day when he'd made contact with the partisans. As a Polish Jew he was no stranger to anti-Semitism, but he'd expected a different attitude at a time when the country was occupied by a common enemy. But he realized at once that nothing had changed. At least not with these partisans. After telling them the purpose of his mission he was asked whether he had any weapons. He produced his revolver. It was taken from him and he never saw it again. "We'll make better use of it," the leader had told him. "You Jews are not fighters, you're merchants."

When had he heard *that* before? "Give us a chance and you'll see whether we can fight or not."

"We don't need your help. We can fight our own battle. We know what fighters you Jews are. At the first sign of danger you'll run the other way."

"And with full pants," one of them had added and earned himself a burst of laughter.

"The Jews are good for two things," another volunteered, "business and praying to your God." And that he illustrated with mocking gestures of a Jew twirling his earlocks.

The leader got into a huddle with two other partisans, then turned to Feivel again. "This is a German revolver. Where did you get it?"

"We bought it from a Pole for five thousand zlotys."

"How do we know you're not a spy sent in by the Germans to discover our base?"

"I'm a Jew. I want to destroy my enemy, not spy for him." He showed them the vial of ciankali. "You know what would happen to me if the Germans caught me outside the ghetto. That's why I carry this with me."

"What else do you have?"

"A few zlotys to get me back to the ghetto."

They'd searched him from head to foot and the only other thing they found was the Star of David armband.

Then he was escorted to the edge of the forest and let go.

He'd made it back to town late that afternoon in time to slip on his armband and rejoin his work brigade just as it was lining up to be marched back to the ghetto.

Having lost their only weapon and the hope of joining the Home Army partisans, the underground had decided to continue their search for weapons but in the meantime to fashion their own. That was when they began making hatchets and storing gasoline.

Three months later they were still unable to obtain a single revolver. As they assessed their situation in the light of today's "action" they found that they had lost, in addition to Isaac, the male orderly, who was also a member, several young women who were grabbed off the streets to fulfill the quota of four hundred the Germans had set for themselves. From all the news they had about other ghettos in neighboring towns they knew that their days were numbered, and that from now on they must make themselves ready for the day when the Germans, together with their helpers, the local fascists, would march in to liquidate the ghetto.

When Hershel and Lena returned to their room, they stayed up long into the night talking about what was uppermost in their minds—little David. They now knew that his only chance for survival was on the Aryan side. But whom did they know on the Aryan side who would be willing to care for a Jewish child for the duration of the war? There were a few Jews in the ghetto who, with the right contacts and for enormous sums of money, were able to find shelter with Polish families. But they had no such contacts and no such money.

At one point Hershel said, "Right now I can think of only one Pole who might by sympathetic to our problem, and if he can't do anything himself, he would probably help with some good advice. That's Pan Bielowski, the architect."

"That's the man who told you to take along a barrel."

"And invented a loose connection in his office so that I could get home a little earlier that famous Friday."

"You haven't mentioned him in a long time."

"I haven't seen him in a long time."

"Then how will you get in touch with him?"

"He's with the Housing Department. I'll have to find a way of getting a message to him. Well, at least we've got *someone* to get in touch with."

At this moment there was a light knock on the door. It was Dr. Weiss. He excused himself for knocking so late. "I merely wanted to ask you a favor," he said to Hershel, remaining at the door. "As you know they took away Isaac, who was also our water carrier. Would you please get us a barrel of water before you go to work. It'll take a day or two before the *Judenrat* will send me a replacement."

"I'll get the water, doctor."

"The barrel is in the kitchen. And you don't have to stand in line. Just tell the policeman you're from the hospital and he'll let you through at once."

It was a good thing the hospital had that privilege. Had he had to wait his turn his work brigade would have gone off without him. As it was he came huffing and puffing to the main gate.

He was still in the railway yard, loading and unloading, doing the kind of manual labor that hadn't the slightest connection with his special skill. On days like today it had its advantage. It left his mind free to concentrate on the urgent problem of getting in touch with the architect. He began with composing a message. After trying several versions he settled on this one:

Dear Pan Bielowski:

> *About that loose connection you wanted me to fix for you, I'll be glad to do it any time you are ready. I am at present*

61

*working in the railway yard and have my tool box
with me.*

The electrician.

He considered mailing it to him but when he gave
it some more thought decided against it. There was
no telling into whose hands the letter might fall. The
Germans might have a man in the Housing Develop-
ment to keep a watchful eye on things. An unsigned
letter without a return address was bound to arouse
suspicion. No, it must not be mailed. It must be
delivered by someone trustworthy and given only to
Bielowski.

There were several Polish workers in the yard's repair shop who did some bartering with the ghetto Jews.
For a handsome reward he could no doubt get one of
them to deliver the message. But he soon realized that
this too could be a step in the wrong direction. Receiv-
ing a cryptic message from a total stranger without
any advance warning might make the architect very
suspicious. He might think it was some kind of trap
laid by the ubiquitous Gestapo. And to clear himself
at once he might hand the message back to the man,
saying: "I'm sorry, but I think there's some mistake
here. I never asked anyone to fix a loose connection for
me, and I don't know an electrician working in the railway yard." And that would be the end of his contact
with Bielowski.

This left only one possibility, telephoning. And it
would have to be done by him. Any other caller would
arouse the same suspicion as a messenger. He knew
there was a public telephone in the station's waiting
room. But that area was forbidden to the ghetto Jews.
He could find his moment during the lunch break when
Feivel could do for him what he once did for Feivel—
distract the guard long enough for him to disappear
behind the back wall of the repair shop, slip off his
armband, walk out of the yard and enter the station
as just another passenger.

But he no sooner conceived the plan when he dismissed it. Too much depended on split-second timing. If anything went wrong and he was caught he would be shot for trying to escape. No, he would have to think of something less risky; and he would have to think of it before the lunch break or he would lose a day. And time was precious.

About fifteen minutes before lunchtime a solution presented itself quite by accident. He had obtained permission from the overseer to go to the privy. When he got there it was occupied. He waited a while and the flagman emerged. He was a man in his late sixties and in ordinary times would have been retired on a pension but what with the wartime shortage of experienced railwaymen he was still able to hold on to a job. He was a friendly man and went out of his way to show his sympathy for the Jewish workers. On very cold days he would bring a thermos of hot tea from the station canteen and distribute it among the workers.

He greeted Hershel warmly and, nodding sadly, said, "I heard what happened in the ghetto yesterday." He looked about him and in a lowered voice added, "They'll be paying for it. Their day of reckoning will come." He squeezed Hershel's arm and was about to leave when Hershel said, "May I ask a favor of you?"

"If I can do it, I'll be glad to."

"I have to telephone someone. It's very urgent."

"Give me the number and I'll do it for you."

"Thank you, but I must do it myself."

"You want to go into the waiting room?" the flagman looked at him with astonishment. "How can I help you with that?"

"If you'll be good enough to let me have your coat and cap for just a few minutes."

After a long pause the flagman said, "It's a very risky thing you're trying to do. What if you're caught."

"I must take that risk. It's the only chance I have to save my child."

The flagman deliberated a moment then placed his hand on Hershel's shoulder and, taking a quick look around him, whispered, "I'm an old man, I'll take the risk with you." They squeezed themselves into the privy and the flagman gave him his cap and coat. "I'll wait here," he said. "When you come back knock and call out my name."

Luck was with him. Bielowski was in his office. Hershel took it for granted that the Germans had put a tap on all the telephones in town and so he did not stray from his prepared message. When he'd finished there was dead silence on the other line and he had the eerie feeling that he had talked into a vacuum. After what seemed an eternity Bielowski's voice came through: "I'll try to see you in the afternoon."

10

AFTER HERSCHEL'S CALL Tadeusz returned to his work. His work at the moment was an assignment from the underground Home Army of which he was a member. As an employee of the Housing Department he was in a very strategic position. He had easy access to the population register and housing allotment records and so when a member of the Home Army, whether he was a partisan from the forest or a functionary passing through on underground business, needed lodging, Tadeusz would fix the records so that the name and address that appeared on the man's identification card also appeared on the books of the town's registry. If for some reason there was any suspicion this was the best proof that the identification was legitimate.

Shortly before lunch the day before, Tadeusz had received a call from a man who said he'd just returned from Cracow and had regards from his cousin. They'd chatted a while about Tadeusz's nonexistent cousin then Tadeusz thanked him and hung up. The caller was Konrad, Tadeusz's Home Army contact. Whenever Konrad called, whether it was to give him regards from a cousin in Cracow, or an aunt in Warsaw, or to invite him to his wife's birthday party, the message was always the same—meet me at the coffee shop between twelve and one. The coffee shop was the ideal place for that kind of meeting. At lunchtime it was crowded to capacity and humming with talk. Konrad usually came ahead of time to procure a table for two and hold Tadeusz's place.

The assignment Konrad had given him was about a partisan who was complaining of abdominal pains and had to come to town to be examined by a doctor. He needed a room and the right papers. It was on this assignment that he was working when Hershel called. Now he found himself unable to concentrate on the assignment. No matter how hard he tried to focus on the work at hand this thoughts drifted to Hershel. Only last night he'd said to Irena, "I wonder what happened to the electrician. I hope he was not among the deported." There were already rumors that the deported were no longer alive, that shooting was heard throughout the afternoon about three kilometers outside of town.

Now his question was answered and he was glad to know that the electrician was not among the deported. But he sensed that his desire to see him was connected with what had happened in the ghetto the day before and he wondered what it was he wanted to see him about. He surmised it had to do with work. As an ordinary laborer in the railway yard he was more liable for a deportation than he would be as a skilled electrician. There hadn't been anything under construction for a long time and there was nothing now, but he had an idea. He would inform the authorities that the time had come for a thorough inspection of all the electrical installations, both military and civilian, and, of course, there was no one more suited for the job than that Jew, the master electrician who had done the installation in von Holtzer's headquarters. The Germans like *ordnung* and they may very well fall for it. Anyway, it's worth a try, and if it doesn't work out he'll think of something else.

But what if the reason for the call is something else? A thought occurred to Tadeusz. What if he wants me to help him escape from the ghetto? At this time wouldn't escape be uppermost in a Jew's mind? Yes, he wants me to find a hiding place for himself and his wife.

Suddenly he found himself pacing the floor without remembering when he'd risen from his chair. Pacing and thinking: What could he tell him? Could he tell him, "I'm sorry, but I'm involved in very sensitive

66

work for the Home Army, so sensitive, in fact, that only my wife and one other person, my underground contact, know about it?" Could he say to him, "I'm sorry, but I don't know of anyone I could safely approach about this. And that includes even some of our acquaintances. You see, my wife and I are considered as a kind of odd couple in our circle because of our attitude toward Jews. We had to stop discussing the Jewish question with them, particularly in the light of my underground activity?" Could he tell him that even his contact man from the Home Army had said to him yesterday, "The Jews are no concern of ours," and this at the time when the Germans were carrying out their deportation "action" in the ghetto.

That evening when Tadeusz had told Irena what Konrad had said tears came to her eyes. "And that man boasts that he has never missed mass no matter what the weather," she said bitterly. "Such people go to church with their feet only, their hearts they leave behind, if they have hearts at all."

No, he could not tell him any of this; and neither could he turn his back on him. To be in the underground and to abandon the Jews would be like fighting Hitler and helping him at the same time. But what *could* he tell him? At the moment he didn't know. All he knew was that he would not turn him down, that he would try to help him. He'd heard of Jews hiding out in the country on farms. There was Irena's aunt, Marusia, a widow, and her daughter, who lived in the country on a small farm. Maybe she would be willing to take them in. At least it was safe to approach her. She was very fond of Irena and him too. She was a decent soul. He'd never heard her take off on Jews as others did.

He was at ease now that he'd thought of Aunt Marusia, and he knew that Irena would be glad to go out to the farm and talk to her aunt. And if necessary he would fix some papers for them just as he did for Home Army people. He stopped at the window to see if the car was there. He was lucky. The one car the

Germans allotted to the municipal personnel was always in use. He had to grab it when it was available. He pushed up the window and called down to the driver, "Gustav, it's taken. I'll be down in a minute." Before leaving the office he paused at the door to think what he should do when he got to the railway yard. Where would he and Hershel talk? And there was the driver to consider. He was a new man and Bielowski knew nothing about him. One day, about two weeks ago, he was surprised to find Wlacek gone and Gustav at the wheel. Wlacek, though not a member of the Home Army, was completely trustworthy. Gustav he knew nothing about. He recalled a phrase Hershel had used on the telephone and smiled. The electrician himself had provided the answer, a loose connection. He went back to the drawing board, took the bulb out of the lamp, pulled the socket from the outlet, ran down and hopped into the car, next to the driver. "Railway station," he announced.

"Going on a trip, Pan Bielowski?"

"Going to pick up a Jew who I hope is there. He's an electrician. My drawing board lamp is on the blink. I fooled around with it myself and I think I made it worse. Know anything about fixing a lamp?"

"Nothing," the driver shook his head.

"Well, this Jew is a whiz at such things. Did all the wiring for me for headquarters."

At the yard Tadeusz found the overseer, identified himself as an official of the Housing Department, and said he had come to borrow one of the men. "That's the one," he said, pointing to Hershel carrying a bag of coal the labor gang was unloading. The overseer ordered Hershel to go with Pan Bielowski and return to the yard when he was finished.

"I'll see to it that he gets back on time," Tadeusz assured the overseer.

On the way to the car Hershel stopped off at the repair shop where he kept his tool box and while there wet his handkerchief and wiped the black grime off his face. He got into the car next to the driver and

Tadeusz sat in the back. "I hope you're equipped to fix a loose connection," Tadeusz said.

"I think so," Hershel replied.

Having spoken mainly for the driver's benefit Tadeusz did not say another word to Hershel until they were alone in his office. He told him to take out his tools and scatter them on the floor near the outlet. "I heard it was pretty bad yesterday in the ghetto," Tadeusz said.

"Yes," Hershel nodded.

"Any of your family . . . ?"

"My mother and my in-laws."

"I'm sorry to hear that."

"The Germans said they were taking them closer to the front to work. But who can believe them?"

Tadeusz nodded sympathetically but said nothing. If he didn't know yet why tell him now? he thought. There's always time for bad news.

"Pan Bielowski," Hershel began, tentatively.

Tadeusz put his hands on Hershel's shoulder. "You and I needn't be so formal with each other," he said. "I prefer that you call me Tadeusz."

"If you call me Hershel."

"I will. Now tell me what you want to talk to me about," he half-whispered.

"About my son. I have an eighteen-month old son."

"Then he was born in the ghetto."

"Yes."

"I heard that pregnancies were forbidden in the ghetto."

"That's right. But my wife was already pregnant when von Holtzer issued that decree. Too late for an abortion. So it became a secret pregnancy. And it was a secret delivery. And the boy is still a secret. But we expect the Germans to come back soon for another "action" and we must get him out of the ghetto as quickly as possible. We almost lost him during this one."

"And how will you get a child out of the ghetto? Have you given it some thought?"

"Frankly, no. First we must find someone willing to take him. To care for him till the war is over. We don't want anything for nothing. We have a little savings. Some valuables. The rest we'll pay off after the war." He paused, searching Tadeusz's face for a clue to his response. Tadeusz seemed lost in thought, as though deliberating what to say.

"You want *us* to take your boy?"

"You're the only one we could turn to, Tadeusz. If you can't take him maybe you can find someone who can. Oh, yes, I almost forgot a very important point. My boy is not circumcised."

"You were very far-sighted, to say the least."

"Not so much far-sighted. You learn from other people's tragedies. When my wife was still pregnant, we heard of a Jew who had escaped from the ghetto and almost succeeded. But he was betrayed by his own circumcision. He was arrested and shot. So we decided that if we had a boy we'd not have him circumcised. And now we don't regret it."

"Hershel, if I can help you in any way at all I will. I'll talk it over with Irena, my wife. We'll put our heads together and maybe we'll come up with an idea. That's all I can promise you."

Hershel grabbed Tadeusz's hand with both of his and shook it vigorously. "Thank you, thank you, Tadeusz," he kept repeating, his voice choking with emotion.

"Hershel, I haven't done anything yet."

"You have already done a lot. You have given me hope."

"I have to tell you something, Hershel. Before I heard your request I was certain it was about yourself and your wife that you wanted to talk to me. Especially in the light of what happened yesterday."

"There's hardly a Jew who at one time or another has not thought about escaping from the ghetto. And some, a few fortunate ones, have succeeded. But for the majority it remains an unfulfilled wish. There's a saying in the ghetto: 'A successful escape rests on three

70

things—a good face, a good tongue, and a good purse.' "

"A good face?"

"Yes. A face that can pass for that of a Pole; a tongue that can speak Polish without an accent; and a purse filled with enough money to buy forged papers, to pay for a hiding place, to bribe yourself out of trouble."

"I should think you meet the first two requirements very well," Tadeusz said. "How about your wife?"

"Only one. She speaks Polish fluently but she has black hair and black eyes that are more characteristic of Jews than of Polish women. But that's not the reason why Lena and I are not planning to escape."

"Money?"

"Not that either," he said, shaking his head. He hesitated and at the same time felt conflicted about his hesitation. If he trusted this man with the life of his child why should *he* not trust him all the way? He looked long and deep into Tadeusz's eyes and just *felt* that he needn't hold back. "Tadeusz," he said, instinctively lowering his voice even though they were alone in the room, "what I am about to tell you I would not tell even to a Jew in the ghetto unless I was convinced he was completely trustworthy."

"I am honored."

"My wife and I belong to the underground . . ."

"You have an underground in the ghetto?" Tadeusz asked with astonishment.

"A small underground of about seventy young men and women. The oldest among us is the doctor. At one point some of us planned to escape. Not to go into hiding but to go to the forest and join the partisans. To fight the Germans, our common enemy. Unfortunately our plan came to naught. So we'll remain in the ghetto. And when the Germans come to deport us, we'll resist. We'll do what we can. You can see why I am anxious to get my child out of there as quickly as possible."

"You have weapons?"

"If you can call a few hatchets and some gasoline weapons. We did have a pistol once but that's gone."

"What happened to it?"

"Do we have time?"

"You're in no hurry to get back. Are you?"

"What for, to haul coal?"

Tadeusz rose and looked out the window. "Anyway, the car is gone. So we have to wait till it's back. Go ahead. I'm curious."

Hershel told him about Feivel's encounter with the Home Army partisans, and how he barely got away from them alive. "How do you know they were Home Army?" Tadeusz wanted to know. "There are all kinds of groups roaming the forest and posing as partisans." The location of the forest and the village adjacent to it indeed suggested that it was a Home Army base, still he resisted the thought and wished it were not true. It was painful for him to accept the idea that the underground he was a member of would take away the only pistol from a ghetto underground that had acquired it at such great risk and cost. It was a heinous deed and he would do something about it. The Jews must get their pistol back. He would talk to Konrad and demand that he retrieve the pistol. Either that or replace it. Yes, he would talk to Konrad about it. It was Konrad who had contact with the partisans. For security reasons he, Tadeusz, never met the partisans for whom he fixed the register and housing records.

Then he recalled that only yesterday Konrad had said to him, "The Jews are no concern of ours," and he had second thoughts about talking to Konrad. He would demand to know how he found out about this and that would mean revealing to him the existence of a ghetto underground; it would mean betraying a trust. And that he would not do, certainly not to an anti-Semite. He decided that somehow he must right the wrong himself. "If you were able to obtain a pistol," he said to Hershel, "how would you get it into the ghetto?"

"How did we get the other into the ghetto? One of

our women members who did cleaning and laundry at the SS officers' quarters sewed it into the hem of her dress. It was risky, and she would have paid with her life if she were caught, but she made it. But we've given up on trying to get another pistol. It's almost impossible to get one. In addition to the hatchets and gasoline I mentioned we're trying to get some scraps of dynamite. We have a chemist in our group and he said if he had enough of these scraps he could make a few explosive devices, small bombs or hand grenades. Only the other day we made a small beginning. I found some scraps in the railway yard's repairshop."

"How did you smuggle them in?"

"I'll show you," Hershel said. He picked up the copper "tool" from the floor and, with a quick twist of the hand, separated the two round halves. He then put it together again and handed it to Tadeusz, who examined it from all sides and said, "It looks like some kind of blow torch."

"That's what the guards probably think it is, and I've been lucky so far."

Tadeusz gave him back the "tool" and walked over to the window. "I see the car is back," he said. "Let's take it before it's gone again."

Hershel began to collect his tools. As he was about to put the socket back into the outlet Tadeusz said, "No, no. Better leave it out. We no longer have a loose connection, my friend. We have something more serious than that." He winked at Hershel. "Can you make it look serious?"

"That's easy," Hershel said, and proved it at once. He detached the socket from the cord, exposing the spliced wires. Then he pulled the outlet from the wall, leaving a gaping hole in its place and bits of brittle plaster on the floor. "How does it look?" he said.

"Very serious. Now I really need an electrician," he said, laughing.

Before they left the room Tadeusz said, "I'll talk to the overseer and tell him that I will need you again soon; that if the driver comes for you he should let you

73

go. It may happen tomorrow, or the day after." When they were at the door Tadeusz stopped and, putting his hand on Hershel's shoulder, said, "I'm sorry about that pistol."

11

LATE THAT NIGHT, long past their bedtime, Hershel and Lena were still up trying to figure out a way to smuggle little David out of the ghetto. Tadeusz's promise to him, "If I can help you I will," was the one bright spot in their depressing life. At least it held out a possibility of saving their child. Even Lena, who was generally far less optimistic than Hershel, allowed herself the hope that Tadeusz would not let them down. Everything she'd heard about him from Hershel added up to what Jews in the ghetto called, "a decent Pole," by which they meant a Pole who would risk helping Jews. In occupied Poland this had become the ultimate test of human decency because it entailed the ultimate risk—one's very life.

If Hershel brought home the good news tomorrow, or the day after, they had to be ready with a plan. But at this moment the problem of smuggling out a child whose very existence in the ghetto was illegal seemed insurmountable. There was simply no way of getting him safely past the guards. If he were old enough to walk or run there might be a possibility, but David had to be carried.

Exhausted, and at their wits end, they had decided to give up for the night and try again tomorrow when Dr. Weiss knocked on the door. Though invited in he did not enter but remained in the doorway long enough to apologize to Hershel for coming to ask of him the same favor he'd asked the night before, namely, to get a barrel of water in the morning. "I asked the *Judenrat* for a replacement for Isaac," he explained, "and they promised to send someone. But they didn't. I guess they have more important things on their minds these days." Hershel told him he didn't mind, he'd be glad to get the water tomorrow, and the doctor thanked him and said goodnight.

Hershel was in the middle of undressing when he suddenly changed his mind, put his trousers back on again, stepped into his shoes and started for the door.

"Where are you going, Hershel?" Lena gave him a baffled look.

"To get a drink of water."

"There's water right here in the pot."

"I mean from the barrel."

"This water *is* from the barrel. What other kind is there?"

"I want to take a look at the barrel. Be back in a minute."

"Hershel, you're not thinking of . . ."

"Yes, I am. It's just a thought. That's why I want to get an idea as to the size . . ."

"Hershel!" There was a ring of alarm in her voice. And before she could manage another word he was already on the other side of the door.

When he returned to the room, Lena noticed the pleased look on his face and she didn't know whether to be happy or not. "Well?"

"Funny," he said, "we've had this barrel since '39, since we brought it into the ghetto; and only yesterday I took it to the pump and back and I couldn't remember the size. I mean how deep it is. Lena, without knowing it Dr. Weiss may have solved our problem."

"Hershel," she said, unable to control her impatience, "what do you have in mind?"

"Tell you in a minute." He undressed quickly, turned out the lamp and got into bed. "The size is right. Of that I'm sure," he said, as though having to convince himself of that fact before he revealed his plan. He moved over close to her and from that moment on they spoke in whispers. "If we're lucky," he began, "and Tadeusz's answer is yes, the barrel may be the only way to get him out."

"Hershel, the boy has never been out of the room.

76

He hasn't even seen the sky. He'll be frightened to death. He may start to cry . . ."

"That part is the least of my worries. Dr. Weiss can give him something. Even chloroform him maybe and he'll sleep through it all. Up until the time that I get to the pump I carry the barrel on my shoulder and nobody can see what's in it."

"But at the pump you have to put it down. What happens then?"

"What happens then is what we have to figure out. I have an idea about that too. I noticed yesterday that at that hour there are hardly any Poles at the pump. The two or three that were there were busy bartering with some Jews and the guard didn't interfere. Now my idea is this: If we can get a Pole who lives across the street from the pump to come out for water at the same time with me, and with a barrel similar to mine in color and size, we switch barrels as soon as he fills his up. He rolls mine away and I his."

"And how will you find such a Pole?"

He fell silent. He had the basic idea of taking the boy out in a barrel, as for details he improvised as he went along. "This is a very poor neighborhood," he finally said, "for a substantial sum of money we should be able to find a Pole willing to do it."

"Who's we? Can you walk out of the ghetto and start looking for such a Pole?"

"*I* can't, but Tadeusz can. At this moment I have to assume that if he undertook to help and if his offer was sincere he'll help all the way."

"All right. So he finds the right Pole, and you're both at the pump; what if, God forbid, somebody notices it? I mean the switch you're talking about."

"Who could notice it? Either a Jew or a Pole. The guard would have to leave his post to notice it. If a Jew happens to see it, I'm not worried. And if a Pole sees it . . . well, we'll simply have to work fast so nobody sees it. Besides, it can't all be done on the first day. We'll have to practice switching barrels filled with

77

water until we feel we're ready. It may take a week even."

"*Oi,* Hershel," Lena sighed. "The way you answer every question it sounds logical. Still my heart trembles with fear about this plan."

"Mine isn't exactly calm; do you have a better plan?"

"If I had, would I keep it a secret?"

They were silent. Hershel became aware of her sobbing. He put his arm around her and pulled her close to himself. They had nothing to say anymore. They had exhausted both the subject and themselves. From sheer exhaustion they fell asleep.

In the morning when Hershel went for water he lingered a while at the pump to survey the scene. The guard and the Jewish policeman at the gate were chatting and smoking. At the pump there were two Poles, both women and both with pails. As he was rolling his own full barrel back to the gate he noticed a young Pole coming out of the first house, carrying his barrel jauntily on his shoulder. Who knows, he thought, maybe that will be the one.

After depositing the barrel in the corner of the kitchen he knocked on Dr. Weiss's door. "I have a favor to ask of you, Dr. Weiss," he said. "I would like to continue getting the water for the hospital."

"Even after I get a new orderly?"

"Yes. For a while at least."

"Why not?" the doctor said, shrugging. "If that's what you want, the favor is granted."

12

THE NEXT DAY, early in the afternoon, Tadeusz called down to the driver, telling him to go to the railway yard and pick up the electrician. "Tell the overseer I sent for him and he'll let him go. I hope he can finish the job today," he added. "I can't work without my lamp."

Twenty minutes later they were alone in the room and as soon as Hershel's tools were spread out on the floor Tadeusz said to him in a voice slightly above a whisper: "My wife and I were up most of the night yesterday, talking about your son. In the end we decided it would be too risky to approach others, even close friends, about taking him in. It's a touchy business. You can't tell what the response would be. If the reply is no, we're already compromised. And that's something we cannot afford—to be compromised. Especially I. You see . . . I am, what you might call, in a very sensitive position. . . ."

"I know what you mean. You're working for the administration."

"Yes," Tadeusz nodded, though that was not at all what he meant. What he meant was his work for the Home Army. "So," he went on, "we decided to take him ourselves."

"*You* are going to take my son?"

"Yes."

Hershel's eyes filled with tears and there was no holding them back. "I don't know how to thank you," he said, his voice shaking and barely audible.

"You can thank me by wiping your eyes," Tadeusz said. "If somebody would walk in here now we'd both be in trouble. Tears are catchy," he said, reaching for his handkerchief and wiping his own eyes while Hershel was wiping his. "Well," he continued, "we have some business to talk over."

"Yes," Hershel said, eagerly. "As I told you yesterday, we have some savings and some valuables and . . ."

"That's not what I meant, Hershel," Tadeusz interrupted him. "We are not doing this for money."

"But the upkeep, at least. You're not rich . . ."

"Hershel, we are doing it because we want to do it. And there'll be no more talk about money," he said, firmly. "Whatever you have, you'll need more than we do."

"Then I insist that after the war I'll pay for all the expenses."

"We can settle that after the war. Now let me tell you about our plan. Since we cannot out of the blue, Irena and I, become the parents of an eighteen-month-old baby your son will be a foundling. There are many such around these days. There's hardly a day without some infant being left on someone's doorstep. The German soldiers impregnate our girls and then disappear. *Deutsche Kultur*. These infants usually end up in the orphanage shelter or in the nunnery. But we'll keep this one. Being a childless couple our decision will be easily accepted by our neighbors and friends. Then we'll proceed with the next step—adoption. You run a notice in the paper for three days, announcing the discovery of a foundling on your doorstep. If after that time nobody comes forth to claim the infant you are legally entitled to adopt it. That's the procedure. And, of course, the boy will have to be baptized so that he can be registered with the church."

"Does he *have* to be baptized?" Hershel asked, hesitantly.

"I can't see how it could be avoided. We're both devout Christians, Irena and I. We go to church regularly. The priest knows us well. It'll look peculiar to adopt a child and not have it baptized. Peculiar and suspicious. It's for the boy's protection and ours."

"You're right. Absolutely right."

"Maybe you want to talk it over with your wife?"

"No. That's not necessary. I know she will agree. After all, that's the reason we didn't have him circumcised. To save his life."

"By the way, what's your boy's name?"

"David. After my father."

"We'll have to find a more Polish-sounding name. How about Dobek? David. Dobek. Close and yet different. Anyway, that's the least of our problems. How will that "foundling" land on our doorstep? That's the problem. I don't mean literally. I mean how will you get him past the guards?"

"We too were up most of the night, Lena and I, and we came up with some kind of plan. It's complicated and risky, but less risky than some of the others we considered." He paused, looked directly at Tadeusz and smiled. "Remember you said yesterday that we were far-sighted about the circumcision? Well, you, it turns out, were even more far-sighted than we were. You told me to take along a barrel to the ghetto."

"I did?" Tadeusz looked perplexed.

"On a Friday in November 1939. The day before we were marched into the ghetto. A day I shall never forget."

"Oh, yes," Tadeusz recalled. "Because of where the pump is located."

"It's in that same barrel that I intend to take him out," Hershel said, and proceeded to unfold the entire plan to him. When he'd finished Tadeusz was silent and the grave expression on his face gave no clue to his reaction one way or another.

"It's the best I could think of," Hershel said, defensively.

"It's a daring plan," Tadeusz finally spoke up, "but it has possibilities if . . ." he sighed, "we can solve two basic problems—find the right man and the right place to billet him in. By the right man I mean someone who's both trustworthy and young and alert enough to have good reflexes. That exchange of barrels you're talking about must take place in split-second timing."

"That's what Lena's worried about."

"Aren't you?"

"Worries the life out of me too. But I figured with practice it could be done."

"Yes, if the man is quick and alert. Now as for billeting him . . ."

"My idea was that the man already lives in the house."

"That would be ideal. But supposing he doesn't? That means you have to bring someone in from outside and find him a room. By the way, can you tell me something about those houses. I haven't been to Glub Street in some time."

"There are three on that half a street. All of them one-story houses."

"You know the number of the first house, the one closest to the pump?"

Hershel thought a moment. "Seventy-something. Seventy-one or seventy-three."

Tadeusz jotted down the numbers on a piece of paper and stuck it in his pocket. "These houses run two apartments to a floor, if I recall, front and back."

"Yes."

"We must concentrate only on the ground floor, which limits us to two apartments to a house."

"Why only the ground floor?"

"Because it stands to reason that only ground floor tenants would come out with their barrels for water. Those who live one flight up will come with pails and fill their barrels that way."

"I must admit I didn't think about that," Hershel said, somewhat embarrassedly. "You know something, Tadeusz, you'd be a great asset to the underground. You see all angles of a problem."

"Think the Home Army would take me?" he said, winking mischievously.

"They'd grab you, provided you don't tell them you're helping Jews."

"After what you've told me I'd keep my mouth shut. To come back to the plan. So we are limiting ourselves to the ground floor apartments. And our preference is for the first house, because it's closest to the pump. Later in the afternoon I'll take a walk to Glub Street and see what I can find out. We'll take it step by step." He glanced at the scattered tools on the floor. "I think you better clean up now. I mean put things together again and leave my lamp in working order. I'll announce that the job is finished. We can't over-play that loose connection bit. That, too, can arouse suspicion."

"How will we get together again?"

"When I have something concrete to tell you I'll get in touch with you. I'll either send the driver or come myself. I'll figure out some reason. Maybe a general inspection of all electrical installations. Maybe my lamp broke down again. We'll see. It'll not be tomorrow, or the day after. We're getting to the heart of the plan. The room. The man. It'll take time. A week. Maybe more." He rose and went to the window. "He's there now. How long will it take you to get ready?"

"About fifteen minutes."

"Then I'll tell him to hold it. Gustav," he called down to the driver, "don't go away. He'll be ready in about fifteen minutes."

As soon as Hershel had left Tadeusz went into the Bureau of Records, a few doors away from his office, and pulled a thick, leather bound ledger off a metal shelf. He ran his finger down the double-entry columns till he came to 73 Glub Street and found that it was, indeed, the first of the three houses. He also found that according to the housing survey conducted by the Germans in March 1940, six months after the occupation, the apartment on the ground floor, back, was occupied by a Czymanowsky family, consisting of a widow, a son, and a daughter-in-law. When he returned to his office he jotted down this information on a Housing Department letterhead and stuck it in his briefcase.

He glanced at his watch. It was 4:00 P.M. He looked out the window. The car was gone. Good, he thought, now is the time to go. On underground missions he always managed to elude the driver, and though this was not a mission for the Home Army it was certainly underground. He put on his brown leather coat, his brown leather cap, picked up his briefcase, and hurried out of the office.

It was a typical April day. The sun was in and out of clouds, sweeping across a blue sky. One moment the sky threatened rain and the next moment the threat was off. Gusts of wind rose as if from nowhere and just as suddenly disappeared, leaving the air calm and pleasantly cool. Tadeusz walked briskly, choosing side streets where neither the staff car nor any inspector on foot was likely to appear.

Glub Street was quiet and, except for a few children playing around the pump, practically deserted. The only other sign of life—if it could be called that—was on the other side of the barbed wire fence where skeleton-like figures, wrapped in tatters, moved aimlessly about, Some, seeing him, pressed their pale, drawn faces against the fence. There was a single German guard in front of the gate, who paid no attention to him. But the children did stop their playing long enough to follow him with their eyes until he disappeared into the hallway of the first house.

Tadeusz knocked several times before someone came to the door. It was a short, frail-looking woman in her late fifties, wearing a brown bathrobe which she held together with her hand. Her graying hair was somewhat disheveled and she looked sleepy. She had obviously just come out of bed. "Are you Pani Czymanowsky?" he asked.

"Yes," she nodded, viewing the stranger with suspicion.

"I am an inspector from the Housing Department. May I come in?"

"An inspector?" she looked at him anxiously.

"Just to ask a few questions. Nothing serious," he smiled reassuringly.

She stepped aside and opened the door wide to let

him in. "My house is untidy," she said, self-consciously. "I'm not well and don't have the strength to clean as I used to. Bad arthritis," she held out her gnarled hands to him.

"I didn't come here to inspect your apartment, Pani Czymanowsky, but if I did I'd give you an A for neatness," he said, glancing around the kitchen.

"Thank you, thank you, Pan Inspector," she said, pointing to a chair, then sat down on the one next to it. Tadeusz opened his briefcase and pulled out the sheet of paper. He studied it a moment and said, "According to our records, Pani Czymanowsky, you occupy three rooms. Two more in addition to this one."

"Yes. A bedroom and a living room. But my bedroom is such a mess right now."

"I'm not going into any of your other rooms," Pani Czymanowsky," he set her at ease. "Our records also show that there are two more occupants in addition to yourself, a son and a daughter-in-law. Are they at work now?"

"My son and my daughter-in-law," the woman nodded sadly. They are at work but who knows where. I haven't seen them in nearly a year," she started to cry.

He waited for her to calm down then said quietly, "Germany?"

"Yes," she sighed. "They went to work one morning and never returned. Caught in a roundup. My son is a master carpenter and they make him work in a coal mine, in a place called Bavaria. And my daughter-in-law works on a farm. They separated them."

"Do you hear from them?"

"Once in a while. The last letter from my son was two months ago. I hope I live to see them again," she said, dabbing her eyes.

"I'm sure you will, Pani Czymanowsky." He paused and glanced at the paper again. "In the meantime you are occupying three rooms all by yourself, which, as you know, Pani Czymanowsky, is against the law. There's a housing shortage."

"Have I done something wrong?" she said, looking at him tearfully, like a child trying to stave off punishment by crying in advance.

"You were supposed to notify the housing bureau of two vacancies, and you haven't."

"I'm an old, sick woman, Pan Inspector," she pleaded. "Please don't throw me out of my home."

"I will not throw you out of your home, Pani Czymanowsky. You will live right here. But we also have to satisfy the law. Let's see if we can work out something that would satisfy both you and the law."

"Thank you, Pan Inspector," she said appraising him with that special wartime shrewdness of an occupied people. He was an official working for the Germans so he should be mistrusted. But he was also a Pole, a son of Poland, who might have some feelings for his own. Still, an official was an official and she hadn't yet met an inspector who didn't want his palm greased. And so while Tadeusz turned to his sheet of paper, as though it held a solution to the problem, Pani Czymanowsky tiptoed into her bedroom and returned with a piece of jewelry in her hand, a heart-shaped gold locket. She placed it on the table, in front of him, and when he asked, "What's this?" she replied, "For your kindness, Pan Inspector."

"That's not necessary, Pani Czymanowsky." He moved it toward her, as though the mere sight of it offended him.

He thinks it's not enough, the woman decided. Because it's small. "It's pure gold, Pan Inspector. It's worth good money."

"I won't accept it even if it were pure diamond, Pani Czymanowsky. I do not accept bribes. I'm not that kind of inspector."

She looked at him as though he were from some other planet. An inspector who didn't accept bribes! Who ever heard of that? "God will reward you for your goodness, Pan Inspector. Will you have some tea, at least, with some homemade preserves?"

86

"That kind of bribe I will accept, Pani Czymanowsky," he said, smiling at her.

She picked up the locket to take it back to the bedroom. "Got it from a Jew across the street," she said, looking at it musingly. "That was when the Germans let us come in to the ghetto to barter with them. We gave them food, they gave us old clothes, bedsheets, jewelry. Now that I'm all alone I live on that jewelry. Sell it off piece by piece."

"Is that all you're living on?"

"That and the little savings my husband left me. My husband was a railway man."

"So he couldn't have left you very much."

"But he was a good man. A very good man." Her eyes grew moist. "Excuse me," she said, and went to put away the locket.

While she was out of the kitchen he noticed the water barrel near the door. He rose and examined it for depth. It was a fullsized barrel. Right now it was almost empty. By the time she returned he was back in his chair.

As she poured the tea she apologized for not having anything more to offer than preserves. She hadn't baked anything since Christmas, she told him. You can't bake without eggs, and who can afford eggs these days. When her husband was alive, he brought home something from every trip. A few eggs. A little butter. Sometimes even a live chicken . . .

"How did he manage to get these things?" Tadeusz was curious

"He was a freight man," she explained. "Sometimes it was an overnight trip and sometimes he was away for several days. Freight trains stop in the middle of nowhere. Farms. Villages. He'd pick up some passengers going from one village to the next. He never took money from them. As they say, 'One hand washes the other.' "

"When did he die?"

"In the winter of '40. Several months after the occupation. It happened in the middle of the night. The train was on the way to Piotrkow-Tribunalski when it jumped the tracks. They say it was the partisans. They mined the tracks. The engineer was killed outright. My husband was badly hurt. Maybe if they had gotten him to a hospital in time they might have saved him. But it was in the middle of the night and in the middle of nowhere. It was not till the morning that they got him to the Piotrkow hospital. But it was too late. He lived for a few more days. Died somewhere alone in a strange place. . . ."

"That must have been a mistake," Tadeusz said. "Partisans aim their sabotage at German troop trains or trains carrying military equipment."

"That's what people said at the time, that it was probably a mistake. But the mistake cost my husband's life."

He felt genuinely sorry for this woman who was now sobbing quietly and whose tears, too, were genuine and not calculated to arouse his sympathy. At this moment he wished he didn't have to play the role of Pan Inspector but could tell her openly why he had come and what his aim was. She had mentioned the partisans without any bitterness even though they were indirectly responsible for her husband's death; and she had mentioned the Jews to an "official" without echoing the German propaganda that they were to blame for the war and for Poland's misfortunes, as many other Poles did. That was why he felt like a hypocrite and a deceiver playing the part he was playing. And yet he knew that for the sake of the plan's success, and even for the woman's own protection, he had to maintain his role throughout and not allow himself to be swayed by these personal sentiments.

When she had stopped sobbing and wiped her eyes dry, he said, "Pani Czymanowsky, I will try to do something for you that will save your home but you must not mention this to a soul."

"I'll do as you tell me, Pan Inspector," she looked at him gratefully.

"You will take in a boarder for a while. A few weeks,

88

a month maybe, and that will make it possible for me to fix up the housing records so that you'll not be bothered again."

"Where will I find such a boarder, Pan Inspector?"

"There are plenty of boarders these days. I'll find one for you."

"A nice, respectable woman?"

"I'm afraid it'll have to be a man, Pani Czymanowsky. One of the laborers who come from the country to work in town. But I'll see to it that he's a respectable man. No riffraff. And I'm sure the rent will come in handy. By the way, what do you charge a month?"

"I've never had a boarder before. People are not eager to rent in this neighborhood. You say it's for a short time. Anything will do."

"Will ten zlotys a week do?"

"That's forty a month. Goodness! That's a lot of money."

"I hear that's what some people get."

"Not in this neighborhood. If he's a poor laborer, twenty-five a month will do."

"We'll see. And he'll help out a bit. Fetch you some fresh water every day. I see your barrel is almost empty. Must be difficult for you to get your own water."

"My neighbor next door gets me half a barrel and it lasts me for two or three days."

"You'll get fresh water every day while your boarder is here. And your neighbor can take a rest." He glanced at his watch and rose. "I'll be on my way now," he said, holding out his hand to her. "You'll hear from me as soon as I have the right boarder for you. I don't want to send you just anyone."

"God bless you, Pan Inspector," she said, seeing him to the door.

As he emerged from the dim hallway into the sudden glare of the afternoon sun Tadeusz glanced cautiously to his right before turning left. It was an instinctive, precautionary gesture. Not that he expected to find here anyone of the municipal personnel, least of all an inspector. Glub Street was one of the town's forgotten streets even before the erection of the ghetto. Its houses were too far gone in their state of dilapidation to be worthy of an inspector's attention. And now that the Germans were warning the Poles to stay away from this area because the ghetto was rampant with typhus (a device to paint the Jews as breeders of disease and thus further isolate them from the rest of the population), Glub Street was shunned by all who had no good reason to be there. Still, he had to come away satisfied that he was not seen by anyone who knew him.

There was a little more life now on the street. People were drifting home from work, or from shopping. Several women, their pails full, stood around the pump talking. The same children were still playing but a little further down the street; and the same guard was still walking his beat at the ghetto gate and looking as bored as before. The figures inside the ghetto, pressing against the fence, looked lifeless. He felt like waving to them, making some gesture of sympathy; but that would only call attention to himself. Looking at them he was suddenly gripped by a sense of excitement at the thought that only a few steps away, beyond that fence, there was a little boy who might soon be in his house, and and that two young Jews were pinning their hopes on him to make that possible. And he had just taken the first step in that direction and it augured well for the rest of the plan.

But that was only one boy; one little boy out of many. And what about the others, so dwarfed by hunger it was hard to tell their age; following with their lifeless eyes the games the Polish children were playing. Was there anyone in this town planning a rescue for them? Not the women standing around the pump; not the men hurrying home from work; not even Konrad, his Home Army contact. If he once had any qualms about posing as an inspector for a private undertaking they now fell completely away. This was not a private undertaking because it shouldn't have to be, and the

90

fact that it was saddened him and filled him with a determination to carry it through.

He glanced at his watch. It was half-past five. He knew Irena was home now. He was eager to tell her about his successful visit with Pani Czymanowsky and to plan the next step. He was too excited to go back to the office. He went straight home.

13

SUNDAY. Tadeusz and Irena had risen at six to attend first mass and after a hurried breakfast of black bread, kylbasy, and tea they hurried to the depot to catch the 8:30 bus to the country. For two days after his visit to Pani Czymanowsky they had grappled with the problem of the "boarder" and had come to the conclusion that it would have to be an out-of-towner, a total stranger. This would fit in with the current pattern of farmhands and other country people coming to town to work on wartime projects, and it would avoid the pitfall of a native being recognized by a Glub Street resident.

Once that decision was reached the natural person to turn to was Irena's aunt, Marusia. She was one of those rare Poles whom they never heard utter an anti-Semitic remark; and though Marusia had never mentioned it herself her daughter, Nina, once intimated to Irena that an entire Jewish family, a husband, wife, and two children, had once been sheltered temporarily on the farm until they found larger quarters. The husband, a dairyman in a nearby town, used to buy dairy products from Aunt Marusia. Thanks to Marusia's willingness to take them in, they had succeeded in escaping from town one day before the other Jews were put into a ghetto.

Irena had heard about this so long ago that she'd forgotten the details of that fragmentary conversation with Nina, and on her subsequent visits to the farm it was never mentioned again. But ever since that time she always looked upon her aunt with a special sense of pride. And there were times when she felt like embracing her and saying, "I know what you've done, Auntie, and I love you for it."

As they left the main road where they got off the bus and came to the narrow path in the field that led to the farm, Irena said, as though to herself, "It's so quiet and restful here you can almost forget there's a war on." Tadeusz, who was lost in thought and had listened mechanically, scanned the horizon dutifully and was about to say something, found himself instead waving to Marusia who had spotted them from her doorstep and was now coming toward them. She was a large-bodied, full-faced woman in her early fifties, whose premature gray hair gave her a much older appearance. Presently she had her arms around them, greeting them with genuine warmth.

"Forgive us, Auntie," Irena said, "but we had no time to let you know we were coming."

"Forgive you for what, for such a pleasant surprise? I'm so happy you came. And one surprise deserves another," she added excitedly. "You've come just in time to meet Nina's new boyfriend."

"Nina's boyfriend? For heavens sake! Since when?"

"Since about . . . let me see . . . about six weeks ago."

"She didn't mention a word about it in her last letter."

"She wasn't sure then."

"Now she is?"

"Now she's up to here in love with the fellow," Marusia held her hand above her head. "Walks around in a dream half of the time."

"What's his name?"

"Lutek. Very nice man. You'll like him."

"Is he here now?"

"Not yet. On Sundays he comes around eleven and stays for the rest of the day."

"In that case, Auntie," Tadeusz said, "we'd like to talk to you about something before he comes." His tone was so serious it prompted her to ask: "You're not in any trouble, are you?"

"No, no. It's just that we want to talk to you alone. It's something just between us."

"Come on in the house. Nina is still dressing. She'll be down soon. But if it's only for my ears we can go in to my room."

"Nina is family," Tadeusz said. "It's this Lutek I had in mind. He may be her boyfriend but he's still a stranger."

They seated themselves around the round kitchen table and though they were all alone Tadeusz, without even thinking about it, fell into a low voice, barely above a whisper, as he unfolded the rescue plan before Marusia, who kept nodding understandingly as he talked. When he was through, there were tears in her eyes. "You two are doing the Lord's work," she said. "I'm glad you came today when Lutek will be here. He can help you much quicker than I can. He knows the countryside and who would do what." She saw the hesitant look on their faces and added, "It's all right. I know he's a stranger to you, but you can trust him. On my say-so you can trust him. He's doing what you are doing."

"He's helping Jews?" Tadeusz asked cautiously.

"I know for a fact he has done so. Yes."

Tadeusz turned to Irena, "Maybe we did come on the right day."

"Tell me more about him, Auntie," Irena said eagerly. "Is he from around here?"

"He's not from this village, if that's what you mean."

"Is he from this area?"

"Now he is. Yes."

"Where was he before?"

"He used to be somewhere near Cracow."

"And he moved here."

"Yes."

"How did he and Nina meet?"

She hesitated. "I'm not supposed to tell you this," she said, smiling self-consciously, "but I'm going to any-

94

way. You're family and if he trusts me he should trust you, too. Lutek is a partisan. He and his detachment used to be in a forest near Cracow, but something bad happened, something very bad. They were betrayed by one of their own men."

"An informer, I suppose," Tadeusz commented.

"Yes. And they had to leave that place. Clear out of there fast. They came to this forest about two months ago. They're still not settled. They're not yet sure they'll remain here. Nina's worried they might move elsewhere."

"I'm still curious to know how they met," Irena said.

"She didn't have to go out looking for him. He walked right into the house. One evening there was a knock on the door and in walked these two bearded men. I'd never laid eyes on them before so I knew they were not from around here. 'We're partisans,' they said. 'Would you mind giving us something to eat?' Well, they ate like they hadn't eaten in days. When they saw we were friendly, they talked about themselves. They admitted not everyone gave them such a friendly reception. Some were afraid the Germans would find out they had partisans in their home; some gave them something because they were afraid to refuse. Anyway, it got late and rather than let them grope their way back to the forest, we offered them the barn for the night and they stayed over. The next day Nina didn't stop talking about Lutek, the younger one. Tadek, the older one, is also very nice but she and Lutek hit it off right away. And he's been coming back ever since. The forest isn't too far from here. It begins at the end of the field. So remember, I've revealed to you a secret."

"Don't worry, Auntie," Tadeusz said, "we won't tell a soul. I, too, would help the Home Army in any way I could." It's as far as he allowed himself to go in revealing *his* secret.

"Lutek happens to be People's Guard," Marusia said. Mention of the People's Guard brought an instant change of expression on Tadeusz's face. It was as though he had been given some bad news. Irena did not look any happier.

"Is there anything the matter?" Marusia asked and, appraising them shrewdly, gave her own reply: "I think I know what's bothering you. It's because Lutek is with the People's Guard, isn't it?"

"That's right, Auntie," Tadeusz said. "They're a left-wing outfit."

"And we support the Home Army," Irena added.

"So do I," Marusia said. "I support anyone who fights the Germans. You can't say the People's Guard is not fighting the Germans, can you?"

"No, that I can't say," Tadeusz admitted. "But I still don't like them."

"Maybe all this is beyond my simple peasant's head," she said, looking perplexed, "but if they're partisans and fighting for Poland I don't care whether they're left-wing, right-wing or middle-wing, if there is such a thing. They fight Poland's enemies, they're Polish patriots. That's what counts with me. Anyway," her grave expression gave way to a smile, "whether you like the People's Guard or not, Lutek you will like. That I promise you."

"As long as Nina likes him," Irena said, "that's the important thing."

"Likes him! These two are already talking marriage! And they've known each other for all of six weeks. So you better like him," she added, smiling. "He's bound to be a relative of yours."

"Still, Auntie," Tadeusz said, in a serious voice, "I prefer not to talk to him about it."

"You mean about the Jewish child?"

"Yes. Let's keep it just between us."

"I think you're making a mistake, Tadeusz, but that's up to you. All I can tell you is I trust him as I trust my own kin."

Tadeusz fell silent. How could he tell her that this was not a matter of trust but of betrayal. To tell a People's Guard man something he deliberately withheld from the Home Army would be an act of betrayal on his part, particularly since it entailed revealing his own specific work for the underground. "It's not that I don't trust him, Auntie," he finally said. "He may be a decent, trustworthy fellow for all I know. It's just that I don't want to have any dealings with the People's Guard."

"You think it makes any difference to that child who saves its life, a Home Army man or a People's Guard man? When your house burns, you don't say, 'I will let only friends put out the fire, all others stay away.' I should think that anyone who comes running with a bucket of water is, at that moment, a friend."

"And that's a simple peasant head talking," Irena beamed proudly at Marusia, leaned forward and kissed her. Then she turned to Tadeusz, saying, "I think Auntie has a point there."

"So you think we should get involved with the People's Guard," Tadeusz looked at her somewhat reproachfully.

"All I say is that we don't shut the door on him before we've even met him. Let's meet him first and decide afterwards. Besides, one man is not the whole People's Guard."

Tadeusz nodded reluctantly, leaving the impression on both women that he was yielding to Irena's suggestion.

Just then Nina walked into the room and, discovering Irena and Tadeusz, let out a cry of surprise and rushed over to kiss them. "My, but we are all dressed up," Irena said, looking admiringly at the freshly ironed white embroidered blouse and flower-printed cotten skirt Nina was wearing, "and I know why," she added, smiling knowingly at her cousin.

"Mom's told you already," Nina said, blushing slightly and, at that moment, looking even younger than her nineteen years.

"Yes, she has. Congratulations. I hear he's very nice."

"Did she tell you what he does?"

"I did," Marusia said. And that he's with the People's Guard," she added hesitantly.

Nina looked rebukingly at her mother.

"It's all right, Nina," Irena said. "We can be trusted."

"I don't mean that. I mean how do you feel about the People's Guard? Some people don't seem to like them. I'm sure you'll like Lutek though."

"I'm sure we will."

Nina glanced at the wall clock. "He should be here soon. I'm going out to see if he's coming. Want to come, Irena?"

"That's right, Irena," Marusia said. "And you, too, Tadeusz. Why don't you all go out and have some of that fresh country air while I get lunch ready?"

They had been scanning the field, stretching all the way to the edge of the forest, and turning their eyes to the narrow dirt roads on either side of them, but a half hour later there was still no sign of Lutek and his horse. "Let's take a stroll," Irena suggested. "Standing around is like watching the pot. It always seems longer. As soon as we walk away, he'll come." She took Nina's arm and her cousin followed her reluctantly, but she kept turning her head back to the house and was too impatient to walk for more than fifteen minutes.

When they returned, they found Marusia sitting on the doorstep. "You look as though the world is coming to an end," she said to Nina. "He's been late before."

"Not *that* late, Mother," Nina said, her eyes brimming with tears. "He's usually here by ten-thirty; it's almost twelve."

There was glum silence. No one had any words of consolation. Lutek was a partisan and therefore exposed to danger. Anything could have happened. They all went inside and while the others tried to make conversation about things unrelated to Lutek and his being late, Nina, slumped in a chair, alternated between staring glumly at the floor and staring at the clock. Around two o'clock Marusia began to set the table. "We'll not bring him here any sooner by starving ourselves," she said.

"I'll help you, Auntie," Irena said, eager to busy herself with something.

Halfheartedly Nina rose and picked up a handful of silver. After placing a setting for Lutek next to hers her eyes grew moist and she walked out of the room. Irena was about to follow her but Marusia held her back. "Let her be," she said. "She'll have a good cry and come back on her own."

Tadeusz was standing by the window, lost in thought. Earlier he had strong reservations about discussing the rescue plan with Lutek. Now he was worried that Lutek might not show up, worried not only for Nina's and Marusia's sake but also for the sake of the plan. Not that he no longer had these reservations. He was still unhappy about the idea of getting involved with a People's Guard man behind the Home Army's back, so to speak.

But how could he dismiss the simple, common-sense truth expressed by Marusia: Does it make any difference to the child and his parents who makes the rescue possible, the Home Army or the People's Guard? But it *would* make a difference if, because of the antagonisms between the two undergrounds, the child fell prey to their mutual enemy, the Germans.

And whose fault is it anyway that he is compelled to consider an alliance not entirely to his liking? If Konrad's attitude toward helping Jews were the same as Lutek's—and he had no reason to doubt Marusia's word that Lutek does "the Lord's work," as she called it—then he would have gone to his own, to Konrad, with Hershel's plan. Thus, recalling Konrad's reaction to the first, large-scale ghetto deportation, and Hershel's story about the only pistol of the ghetto underground, made it easier for him to whittle away the lingering reservations about talking to Lutek.

Suddenly the door was flung open and his train of thoughts was shattered by Nina's almost hysterical cry, "He's coming! He's coming!" And they all ran outside.

After the introductions Irena observed that Lutek looked as she had imagined him to look: Boyish. Open-faced. Sandy-haired. Blue-eyed. Very Polish. And with a ready smile that instantly attracted one to him. She could see why Nina was so taken by him and why Marusia, too, liked him. He had the quality of setting one at ease in his presence. She felt it and noticed with satisfaction that Tadeusz felt it too.

"I hope I haven't kept you waiting with your meal," he said to Marusia.

"You have, and we'll forgive you if you wash up quickly and come right in."

Nina brought out a towel and welcomed the opportunity to be alone with him at the pump. He held his head under the pump's mouth while she worked the handle up and down. The rush of ice cold water on his head nearly took his breath away. As he was drying himself Nina said, "Lutek, you look sad. What happened?"

He looked at her for a long moment before he spoke. "I buried my friend, Tadek, this morning."

"Tadek!" Tears welled up in her eyes. "My heart told me something had happened." She shook her head slowly, looking off into space.

"I almost didn't get here myself."

"Lutek!" Nina barely managed in her choking voice and threw her arms around him.

Marusia appeared on the doorstep and, seeing them locked in an embrace, hesitated a moment then said, quietly, "Soup's on the table, children," and returned to the kitchen.

Marusia noticed that he ate without appetite. It wasn't at all like Lutek; nor was it like him to be so broodingly silent. "Was there trouble again?" she asked.

He nodded somberly.

"Tadek is dead, Mother," Nina said, as though replying for him.

"Tadek! That nice man! Jesus Maria," she crossed herself. "How? What happened?" She saw him hesitating and said, "It's all right, Lutek. Tadeusz and Irena know you're a partisan. I told them."

"And that you're People's Guard," Nina added.

"So you told them about that too," Lutek said, smiling at Marusia.

"They're family."

Lutek turned to Tadeusz and Irena. "There's family and family," he said. "But I take it you're the right kind of family or she wouldn't have told you."

"We think we are, anyway," Tadeusz said.

"You've heard about the informer, I suppose."

"Only that you had one, and I take it he caused you some losses."

"Nearly a third of our detachment! Needless to say we've been looking for that fellow. Well," he continued, addressing himself now to the entire table, "last night we got word from our contact that he's in this area, in a village about eight kilometers from here.

"It didn't seem likely that he would be sniffing around the forest again that soon. Usually, after one of their rats pulls a big job for them the Germans put him on ice for a while, then transfer him to another part of the country, where he's least likely to be recognized, to do his work for them in some city or town. Still, we couldn't afford not to act on the tip. It had to be checked out.

"Tadek and I were picked for the job. We used to go out on missions together and could recognize the fellow even by his voice alone. So we set out early this morning for the village and went straight to the hut where he was seen. It turned out to be a mistake. There was a slight resemblance to the fellow, but he was a relative of the peasant's on a visit.

On the way back we ran into a German foot patrol, an unexpected surprise. They were four and we were two. If they searched us, they would discover our weapons and our goose would be cooked. We had one advantage, we were on horseback, and had to make use of it quickly. We each tossed a grenade at them, turned around, and fled. One of the Germans opened fire and hit Tadek twice. Though he bled badly he managed to hold on till we got to our base. Then he collapsed. We buried him in the forest."

For a moment they all stopped eating and no one spoke. It was as though they were paying a silent tribute to the fallen man. Marusia and Nina who had met Tadek a number of times and liked him brushed tears from their eyes. Marusia broke the silence, saying: No priest . . . no confession . . . no family at the graveside . . ." She turned to Lutek, "Is there at least a marker on his grave?"

"No marker. That could give us away. We made a sign for ourselves though, a small carving on a tree. It'll do until after the war. As for a priest . . ." he paused, deliberating whether to reveal in the presence of Tadeusz and Irena something he had never before mentioned even to Marusia and Nina, something that not all in his detachment even knew. "Marusia," he finally said, "for Tadek a rabbi would have been more in order than a priest."

"Tadek?" Marusia's voice expressed astonishment, "I would never have guessed he was a Jew."

"Neither would I," Nina added. "You certainly couldn't tell from the way he talked. He spoke without an accent."

"That's one of the reasons he was able to escape from the ghetto and make it to the forest," Lutek said. "With an accent even false papers are not of much help."

"You have any more Jews in your detachment?" Irena was curious.

"We had one more, who went by the name of Janusz. In fact, he came to the forest together with Tadek; we lost him in that German trap the informer led our men into. Come to think of it, Tadek, too, fell because of the informer."

"How did they happen to come to your detachment?" Tadeusz wanted to know. "Did they just wander into it, or what?"

"No, they didn't just wander in. They knew where

they were going and we expected them. We'd been in touch with the ghetto underground. Gave them some weapons. Very little because we have to scrounge around for them ourselves. We don't have the kind of supplies the Home Army has. About six had escaped. But only these two made it. The others . . . well, two were betrayed by a peasant who was a collaborator. The other two ran into a German ambush soon after they left town. Tadek and Janusz always volunteered for the most dangerous missions. They said they had a special score to settle with Hitler. If anybody tells you Jews can't fight don't believe it."

"There's a ghetto in my town, you know," Tadeusz began cautiously. He was no longer in doubt about seeking Lutek's help; it was only a matter of how best to broach the subject.

"If we decide to make this forest our base, we'll try to contact that ghetto."

"If you wait too long there might not be a ghetto to contact anymore," Irena said. "The Germans carried through one of their "actions" several days ago . . ."

"I've heard something about it from one of the peasants. Was it in your town?"

"Yes," Tadeusz nodded. "Several hundred Jews."

"Wonder if they have some kind of underground," Lutek thought out loud.

"They have, but no weapons."

"Unfortunately we can't be of much help in this direction. Not now, anyway. We've been bled white. We're trying to get back on our feet."

"There's one way you may be able to help . . ."

"Not weapons . . ."

"No, not weapons . . . advice . . . maybe in other ways . . ."

"Well. what is it about?"

"It's about smuggling a child out of the ghetto, a baby boy." And without any further introduction he began to unfold the entire plan for the rescue of little David. Though Marusia had heard the plan earlier from Tadeusz she listened with the same absorption as though she were hearing it for the first time. And Lutek, a veteran of many daring encounters with the Germans, found the plan so engrossing he kept shaking his head incredibly as he listened and at the end smiled a deeply satisfying smile, as though the partisan in him was both intrigued and gratified by the boldness of the plan. "I see you've got everything planned to the last detail," Lutek said. "All you need is the 'boarder,' as you call him."

"The *right* 'boarder,'" Tadeusz stressed. "Without the right 'boarder' the whole plan remains on paper. And it's got to be someone from out of town. That's the reason we're here today, Irena and I." He paused, looked intently at Lutek and, in a half-serious tone, said, "Now, if you were willing to part with your beard I would say we wouldn't have to look any further. We have our 'boarder' right here."

"That's all that stands in the way," Lutek smiled, "my beard?"

"I don't think your beard would go well on Glub Street. It would make you too conspicuous."

"Are you serious? I mean . . . about me taking the job. . . ."

"I'm serious, if you're serious."

"To tell you the truth I *am* serious. The plan appeals to me."

"I can start working on your papers tomorrow."

"We're not up to that yet. I don't make such decisions on my own. I'll have to speak to the commander. Can you be here next week?"

"I can but a whole week is a long time."

"A week later may be too late," Irena said.

"She's right," Tadeusz agreed. "They're very fearful in the ghetto. The Germans may come again any day."

Lutek glanced at the clock. It was half past three. "I could make it there and back by six," he said, rising.

"If the commander says yes, then I'm going with you," Nina said, emphatically. "I'll stay with them," she nodded toward Tadeusz and Irena.

"You're most welcome to stay with us," Irena said.

Lutek turned to Tadeusz. "How long do you think it'll take? I mean being a 'boarder.' "

"Hard to say right now. Depends on how things go. You have to count on at least two weeks."

"I can't manage here by myself for two weeks, Nina," Marusia said.

"But can I go for a few days, Mother?"

"You can settle that later," Lutek said, adding, "If there's something to settle," and he started toward the door.

They all followed him out of the house and watched him mount his horse. He sat on it motionless for a moment, looking directly at them and smiling, as though posing for a photograph. Then he dug the heels of his spurless boots into the horse's belly and took off.

"Be very careful, Lutek!" Nina called after him, waving. But he gave no sign of having heard her. He was galloping fast across the field, heading straight for the forest.

Lutek returned to the farm shortly before six, bringing the news that the commander had approved his going to town. Tadeusz and Irena were genuinely pleased. While he was gone they spent some time alone, sharing their impressions of him, and came to the conclusion that he would make an ideal 'boarder.' He was courageous, had the right attitude toward Jews, and was trustworthy. Of course, they would have been happier if he were not associated with a rival underground, but this single drawback was more than overcome by his positive qualifications. Besides, they were not dealing here with the People's Guard but with someone who happened to be a member of it. As far as they were concerned this was a strictly private undertaking on their part, something separate and apart from the organization to which he belonged. And he was determined to keep it that way. Yes, they were lucky, indeed, to have found the right man on their very first try.

105

"What about your beard?" Tadeusz said.

"You say it must come off?"

"It should. It'll make you stand out too much. You know yourself, in this kind of work the less your face is remembered the better off you are."

"I hate to part with my beard, but you're right. It should come off. I like your caution. You're alert to details. You know something, Tadeusz, you'd make a good man in the underground."

"Are you trying to recruit me into the People's Guard?" Tadeusz said, smiling.

"As a matter of fact, I am," he nodded, and seeing Tadeusz's smile changing to a wide grin, added, "I'm serious."

"I'm not a candidate," Tadeusz shook his head firmly.

"You don't understand. I don't expect you to leave town and come to the forest. You can do a lot for us just being where you are."

Tadeusz surmised what he had in mind, still he asked, "Doing what, for instance?"

"Doing what you're going to do for me, fixing up papers for some of our partisans whenever the need arises."

"No, Lutek, that's out of the question."

"We already have an address. From now on Pani Czymanowsky won't have to look for new boarders. I can always recommend a 'friend.' In fact, we'd pay the rent even when we don't use the room. Just to keep the address."

"I promised her a 'boarder' for only a few weeks, but that part of it could be worked out. She can use the rent. But I won't do the other."

"But why?"

Tadeusz was silent. He just stood there, shaking his head slowly and staring past Lutek into space.

"I know you'd be taking a risk," Lutek pressed on, "but so am I. Every day. Fighting the enemy involves risks."

"If you question my patriotism, Lutek, you're wrong. I'm as patriotic as the next man, even though I'm not in the forest."

"Then why won't you do it?"

"I have my reasons. And I wish you wouldn't press me on that point because I'm in no position to offer any explanations."

There was a long silence as Lutek looked at him probingly, wondering what those reasons could be. Finally he said, more to himself than to Tadeusz, "I guess I spoke too soon."

"What do you mean by that?" Tadeusz wanted to know.

"My commander was not very keen on my getting involved in this. We're too weak now to take on such missions. I had to talk him into it. I told him it was for the good of the detachment; that you can help us get a foothold in town. Now you come and say you can't do it. Where does that leave me?" There was an unmistaken tone of reproach in that question; and the same was true of the look he gave him. Then he turned around and started to walk away.

Tadeusz hurried after him and took his arm. "You're not backing out of it, are you?" he asked.

"I should, but I'm not."

They walked on in silence, past the farm, with no apparent destination. "I appreciate it," Tadeusz finally said, somewhat apologetically. "Some day, when I tell you why, you'll understand the reasons."

"Some day the war will be over and there'll be no need for explanations and reasons. I'm concerned with now. There's that Jewish kid, of course. But there's also the room at Pani Czymanowsky's, there's the five hundred zlotys, you said the father will pay. They can buy some grenades. I'll have a chance, on good papers to look around town and see what it can do for us if we settle in this area. These are *my* reasons for not backing out. And there's one more reason—you."

"Me?" Tadeusz looked at him with surprise.

"Yes. I don't take your reasons, whatever they may be, as your final word on this matter. I'm hopeful you may still change your mind."

The idea of working for both the Home Army and the People's Guard seemed inconceivable to Tadeusz, but not wanting to hurt Lutek's feelings his reply was deliberately vague: "So you think there's still hope for me," he said, and moved on to a more immediate subject: "How soon will you be ready to move in to Pani Czymanowsky's?"

"I'm ready right now."

"That's a little too soon. You haven't got your papers yet."

"She's expecting a 'boarder,' isn't she?"

"Yes. But she's expecting a 'boarder' who goes to work in the morning. A construction worker. Sitting around the house when you should be at work would look suspicious."

"How soon can you have the papers?"

"Tomorrow, hopefully. I'll work on them lunchtime when some of the others are out. But one can't be sure . . . There may have to be a delay."

"Then what do you suggest?"

"I suggest that only Nina come along with us and wait in my house till I bring her the papers. Then she'll take the first bus out to the farm and you can both return to town on the seven o'clock bus. If things go well all this can happen tomorrow. In the meantime I can also drop in on Pani Czymanowsky and tell her to expect you."

"You've thought of every detail."

Tadeusz smiled, nodding. "While you were gone, I had time to think. I even discussed it with Nina. I had a feeling the commander would say yes."

"And you say you have reasons not to join the underground."

"Lutek, you're recruiting again." He glanced at his watch. "In half an hour we catch the bus. Let's go."

They hurried back to the house.

14

WHILE HERSHEL was waiting for Tadeusz to contact him he did what he could do to advance the plan, and the thing he did was to acquire a barrel which, in size and color, resembled the hospital's water barrel. He lowered little David carefully into it and waited to see what would happen. The boy looked up at him and grimaced, as though he were about to cry. He lifted him out of the barrel, comforted him and a few minutes later put him back into it. Then it was Lena's turn to repeat the same routine. After a while the child got used to standing in the barrel without fear. It became a kind of vertical crib which he did not particularly like but which he learned to accept without protest.

On Tuesday morning when he went for water Hershel noticed a new face at the pump, a young man he had not seen before. Is that the one? Hershel wondered. He watched the stranger scanning the line of waiting Jews as though he were looking for a particular one and, standing near him, he was tempted to ask: "Is it perhaps for me you are looking?" But of course he did not. He knew that before he spoke a word to this stranger he would have to, in some way or other, be introduced to him by Tadeusz, or get specific instructions from Tadeusz how to identify himself to him. When he returned to the hospital Hershel said to Lena: "I think the man we want is here."

"Have you spoken to him?"

"No," Hershel said, looking somewhat dazed by the experience.

"I have a feeling . . . I've never seen him before. Besides, I saw him pump his barrel half full and roll it into the first house. The only other Pole who sometimes comes out with a barrel from that house is an older man. Something tells me I will hear from Tadeusz soon, maybe even today." He put his arms around Lena and held her close. She had tears in her eyes. So did he.

He did not come that day, but the next day, Wednesday, he showed up at the railway yard in the early afternoon. The overseer came running up to him at the loading platform. "Get your tools and go with Pan Bielowski," he ordered. "He needs you."

Hershel expected Tadeusz to be alone. To his surprise Tadeusz led him to the car where the driver was at the wheel, waiting. "We're going to the barracks, Gustav," Tadeusz said, taking the back seat and letting Hershel sit in front with the driver. Not a word was spoken throughout the three-kilometer ride. When they got to the barracks Tadeusz said to the driver, "I don't want to tie up the car for nothing. It'll take some time to inspect all the installations. Come back for us in about an hour and a half. Two at the latest."

Most of the soldiers were away on guard duty or other assignments. The few who lingered in the barracks area were either on sick call or off duty. Tadeusz and Hershel went around "checking" electrical installations until they came upon an empty barracks where they could be by themselves. Hershel spread some tools on the floor and they both crouched down. "We have a 'boarder.'" Tadeusz whispered. "He's already here."

"I think I know who it is. I saw him at the pump."

"He thinks he saw you too. You kept looking at his barrel."

"Was I that obvious?" Hershel shook his head self-deprecatingly.

"It's all right. He did the same thing. He says the two barrels are very much alike."

"That was also my impression."

"Then let's make that the password. Tomorrow, at the pump, he will speak first. He'll say to you: 'Our barrels are very much alike'. And what will you say?"

"I will say, 'They are, indeed, sir.' "

"All right. That'll be the password and from then on you'll be on your own."

"Are you seeing him today?"

"No. I saw him yesterday and the next time I hope to see him again is when it's all over."

"Then how will he know the password?"

"It'll be passed on to him by his girlfriend, who acts as our go-between. She's my wife's cousin. She'll stay with us for the next few days."

"She's not from this town then."

"No. And neither is he. By the way, I promised him five hundred zlotys."

Hershel reached for the copper "blow torch" among his tools, twisted it open and pulled out a bundle of bills tightly pressed together. "I've been carrying it around with me for almost a week to have it ready," he said, handing the money to Tadeusz.

"That's more than five hundred."

"Fifteen hundred. My savings. Please take it all. We still have a few valuables to sell."

"All right, if it'll make you feel better. I'll save the rest for you."

"Will I see you again?" Hershel asked.

"It would be wiser not to. For some time at least. If anything should happen in the next few days, I mean something that I should know, send a message through the man at the pump, the 'boarder.' He's fully trustworthy."

Tadeusz did not volunteer the 'boarder's' name and Hershel did not ask. If anything he was impressed with Tadeusz's caution. It augured well for his son's safety. "How will we know that all went well, that the child was brought safely to your house?" Hershel asked.

Tadeusz thought a moment. "Do you get to see the *Courier?*"

"Yes. The flagman buys it for me at the station."

"Good. Watch the announcements on foundlings. That's how you'll know. In the meantime you'll go by the maxim that no news is good news." He glanced at his watch. "The driver should be back soon. Maybe you should start gathering up your tools."

They were standing by the barracks window, looking out on the road, and they were silent. "So this may be the last time we're seeing each other," Hershel spoke up, ending with a deep sigh.

"The last time for now . . . for the duration of the war perhaps . . . yes." He saw the sad, distant look on Hershel's face and put his arm around him. "We'll take care of your son as though he were our own. I promise you."

Hershel looked long into Tadeusz's eyes, saying more with his silence than he could with words. Then he seized his hand and squeezed it tightly.

"Did you ever think of escaping?" Tadeusz asked.

"With an infant?"

"Well, now you'll be free."

"Not so simple. You've got to have papers. An address . . ."

"How about the forest? You don't need papers for the forest."

"For the forest you need weapons. I told you what happened to our one pistol when we did try to go to the forest."

"Yes," he sighed, "I remember," feeling both shame and indignation rising within him. After a long silence he said, "If you should try again, Hershel, go east instead of west."

"In the opposite direction?"

"Yes. There is a forest there, one hour's ride by bus; and there are partisans there too."

"Home Army?" Hershel asked, hesitantly.

Tadeusz shook his head. "You'll be welcome there."

They heard a quick toot of the horn. "He's here," Tadeusz said, spreading his arms wide. The two embraced as though they were welding themselves to each other. "The best of luck to you, Hershel," Tadeusz said.

"Thank you, friend."

15

THINGS WERE GOING WELL at the pump. On the very day that Hershel and Lutek exchanged passwords they also exchanged barrels, as if to prove to themselves that the barrels were, indeed, similar to each other. The next morning Lutek whispered triumphantly to Hershel, "My landlady didn't notice any difference."

And they managed to exchange not only barrels but also information. From a word, a wink, a half-phrase, a nod, a shrug, they fashioned a language with which to communicate. Soon these bits and pieces of whispered conversation began to assume a meaning beyond the immediate purpose of the child's rescue, and Hershel was able to report to his group in the typhus room that "we now have a trustworthy contact with the Polish underground. This time the forest has come to us to tell us we'd be welcome in the forest."

Someone had asked: "And what about weapons? You can't go to a forest empty-handed."

"I asked the same question and this was his answer: 'As you know, a barrel is not only for water.' "

And so a hope snuffed out was now a hope rekindled.

They had synchronized their time of arrival at the pump so that neither had to wait for the other. When Lutek emerged from the hallway, rolling his empty barrel, Hershel passed through the gate carrying his on his shoulder. They had learned to exchange barrels with such ease and dexterity that the bystanders were unaware of their sleight of hand. And back in their hospital room Lena and Hershel had, with patience and playfulness, converted an object of fear into an odd-shaped toy house. Little David now looked forward with an expectation of delight to being rolled around the room in the barrel, in an upright position, to the accompaniment of singing and hand-clapping.

One week after they had exchanged passwords at the pump Lutek and Hershel agreed that the practice period was over, that they were ready for the final exchange of barrels for which they had been preparing themselves.

"Tomorrow, then," Hershel had whispered, expecting a firm, unwavering yes.

"Day after tomorrow. Tomorrow we'll have a trial run."

"A trial run?" Hershel looked puzzled.

"Don't come out empty," Lutek explained. "Put something in, anything."

Hershel had nodded, eagerly accepting the suggestion, feeling greatly relieved. Lutek had given him a day's reprieve from something he both terribly wanted and terribly dreaded.

After searching their room for something expendable they could use for the trial run they settled for an empty old burlap bag Lena had once brought in from the hospital kitchen. It was the only thing they could spare. As he was approaching the gate Hershel became aware of feeling self-conscious, of casting furtive glances around him, of tension mounting inside him. He had to remind himself that little David was back in the room sleeping, that it was only a burlap bag he was carrying in the barrel. And he was once again grateful to Lutek for having suggested a trial run. He had to learn *now* that calm and composure did not begin at the pump.

He stopped at the gate, his eyes peeled on the house across the street. At this time Lutek was supposed to emerge from the hallway. Instead a woman, carrying a pail, came out of the house and headed straight for the pump. Lutek had apparently overslept, he decided, and thought it ironic that of all days it had to happen on the day he had selected for the trial run.

The Jewish policeman who was in the ghetto underground also participated in the trial run. His job was to keep an eye on the scene at the pump and, at the crucial moment, offer the guard a cigarette and light it for him, thus blocking his view. He now caught a glimpse of Hershel inside the gate and gave him a questioning look. Hershel's reply was a quick shrug that plainly expressed his concern over Lutek's absence.

His concern deepened when fifteen minutes had passed and still there was no sign of Lutek. He could not tarry any longer or he would miss his labor brigade at the main gate. He pulled the burlap bag out of the barrel and threw it to the ground though he knew that as soon as his back was turned it would be gone. He hurried through the gate, filled up his barrel and rolled it back to the hospital, still keeping an eye on the house across the street through the fence.

"Something went wrong, Hershel," Lena said, as soon as he walked into the room. "I can see it on your face."

"He didn't show up."

"What do you suppose happened?"

"Do I know?"

"Is it possible that he overslept?"

"It's possible. If it were only that there'd be no reason to worry."

"What else could it be?"

"I hate to think what else it could be. He could be arrested, for instance. Wouldn't that be bad enough? But before we think of the worst let's see what the rest of the day will bring. If something bad happened, Tadeusz would know about it. They've been in touch through a go-between. And if there's something we should be warned against Tadeusz will find a way of letting me know. He's a responsible person." He saw the distraught look on her face and said, "Then again you may be right. It's also possible that he overslept and tomorrow he'll show up and apologize."

"I hope so. But until tomorrow the day will be as long as a year."

He gulped down the cup of black chicory she placed before him and stuffed the slab of bread into his pocket.

"I'll eat it later," he said, "I'm late." He stopped at the bed for a quick look at his sleeping son, kissed Lena, and was off.

Tadeusz did not show up at the railway yard that day and Hershel and Lena were no wiser in the evening than they were in the morning about the reason for Lutek's absence at the pump. Though their thoughts were full of dark forebodings they kept them to themselves and clung to the one hope they could logically hold on to—Lutek had overslept. It was human. It was possible. And wasn't that the reason why Tadeusz did not try to see Hershel? He had nothing to tell him. As simple as that!

After supper they went through with their nightly routine of putting David into the barrel and rolling him around the room. The child's squeals of delight made them forget their worries for a while. But after the game was over and the child had been put to bed they lapsed into despondent silence, feeling as though they had participated in some futile exercise, fooling both themselves and their child. Hershel reached over to Lena and took her hand. "Mark my words," he said, trying to sound as convincing as possible, "tomorrow he'll be at the pump before me. He'll look sheepish and he'll apologize for oversleeping. Come, let's go to bed."

"You even know how he will look? Let him not look sheepish, and let him not apologize. Just let him show up."

"All right, I'll make that concession. He'll not look sheepish and he'll not apologize. He'll just show up. Satisfied?"

"Yes."

He'd succeeded in forcing a smile on her sad face. A small triumph.

Once again Lutek did not come out to the pump the next morning, and neither did Tadeusz show up at the railway yard. They had to abandon the one hope they had clung to. It was not likely that a man of Lutek's responsibility, a member of the underground, would oversleep two days in a row. Clearly, something had happened; and since they didn't know what, they had to assume the worst, that Lutek was under arrest. And if that were the case the consequences could be serious not only for the fate of their son but also for their own underground. Lutek knew of its existence. No one could predict how one would behave under the strain of Gestapo torture.

Lena invited Dr. Weiss to their room and he was apprised of the situation. "Yes, it does sound serious," he said, nodding gravely. "Of course, it's also possible that the man is lying in his bed right now, across the street, unable to move because of a high fever, or a broken leg or something. Or maybe he was told that his mother was dying and he hurried home to her bedside. These are all valid possibilities. Still, you are right. We must assume the worst and act accordingly. Frankly I don't know whether we're in a position to do anything, but let's discuss it together. Maybe somebody will come up with an idea."

That evening the whole group met in the typhus room. The first reaction to Hershel's report was one of stunned silence. His previous reports of his daily meetings with Lutek at the pump had given them the justifiable belief that they had at last found a reliable contact with the Polish underground, one that might even succeed in getting them some weapons. Overnight that belief seemed to have turned into a threat. But after the initial shock came a more sobering assessment of their situation.

"True," Dr. Weiss began, "there is no question about our helplessness, but there *is* a question about our hopelessness. It is in the nature of man when attacked to either counterattack or flee the scene of danger. We are not in a position to do either. We have no weapons to fight with, and we cannot run from here. In this sense we are, indeed, helpless. Still, this is no reason to let the Germans rob us of the one weapon we do possess —hope.

Another man spoke up: "There may be other reasons

117

why this good man suddenly disappeared. Perhaps even escape from arrest. He's a Pole. He can do what we cannot. And if arrest was the reason it does not yet mean that he's talked. Most underground fighters keep their lips sealed till their very last breath, despite Gestapo tortures. So let's not despair. Not yet, anyway."

Since they could do nothing about their own fate except speculate and hope, they turned their attention to little David. What if the Germans learned of his existence and demanded that he be handed over? Was the typhus room a safer hiding place than the room he was in now? Again, they could only speculate. They knew there was no safe place in the ghetto for anyone, let alone a baby. They decided that if Lutek did not show up in the next two days they would meet again to discuss how the entire group could pool its resources and get behind the scheme of smuggling the child out of the ghetto.

The next morning Lutek was again absent at the pump. But on the fourth day he showed up at the usual time. "I'm sorry to have worried you," he'd managed to whisper, "but I was called away on business. Urgent business," he added with a wink.

"Successful?"

"Yes." He put a cigarette in his mouth and offered one to Hershel. They began lighting up, deliberately having trouble with matches, a device they had used several times before. It made it possible to stand off to one side and hold their heads close to one another without arousing undue suspicion. Between making many unsuccessful "tries," and cursing the poor quality of wartime matches, they managed a brief, whispered conversation. "An informer," Lutek told Hershel. "Been hunting for him for months . . ."

"On this street?"

"On the square. . . . sitting in a car . . . a chauffeur . . ."

"In front of the municipal building?"

"How did you know?"

Hershel was too stunned to reply. He grew pale and his hands trembled.

"Don't worry," Lutek assured him. "He'll not inform on anyone anymore."

"And Tadeusz?"

"He's safe. . . . Sent this message to you: 'No more loose connections. Lamp works well . . .' He said you'd understand."

Hershel smiled, nodding. His natural color returned to his face. His hands stopped shaking.

"Are you ready for tomorrow?" Lutek asked.

"Trial run?"

"No time. The real thing."

"I'm ready if you are."

"I am." As if to prove it he exchanged barrels on the spot, as though nothing had happened in the last few days.

The next morning, about fifteen minutes before little David was to be transferred from the bed to the barrel, Dr. Weiss came into the room, carrying in his hand a piece of cloth soaked in chloroform. He held it close to the child's nostrils for several short intervals before he handed it to Lena to dispose of. "I gave him a light dose," he explained. "Just to keep him asleep for the next hour or so."

"He's never seen the sky," Lena said, as though to herself, while her eyes were glued to David's face.

"Let's hope he doesn't see it on this trip," Hershel commented. "He'll have plenty of time to catch up on sky later."

"You needn't worry about that," Dr. Weiss assured him. "It would take a thunderclap to wake him up before this thing wears off."

"I wish you'd put me to sleep for a while, doctor," Lena said. "I don't know how I'll survive the next half hour."

"If you've survived until now, you'll survive the next half hour also. Come along with me and busy yourself on the ward. Don't remain alone in the room."

"All right, Lena, the time has come," Hershel said in a tone of urgency.

Lena lifted the child from the bed and lowered him gently into the barrel. "Goodby, my treasure," she whispered to her sleeping son. "Remember, we'll always love you and come back for you after the war." Then she turned abruptly, covered her face with her hands and began to sob.

Hershel hoisted the barrel on his shoulder and started for the door. "Good luck," the doctor half-whispered. Lena did not turn around.

There was a bracing coolness in the early morning air. The sun was up and the sky a clear blue. He kept close to the fence, nodding greetings to those he knew, standing in line. From a distance he glimpsed his friend, the Jewish policeman, standing next to the German guard. A reassuring sight. As he approached the gate he deliberately slowed down, keeping a close eye on the house across the street. He was aware of his quickened heartbeat and rising tension and told himself to relax. He told himself. But who listened? Not his heart and not the rest of him. If anything, he felt as though his legs would not take another step. And yet they carried him forward, as though they had taken over and acted on their own. And he was glad they remembered. For there was Lutek, emerging from the hallway with his barrel on his shoulder.

He was midway between the gate and the pump when he heard the German guard shouting, *"Halt! Halt!"* Was it at him the command was directed? If so what was he to do? Where was he to run? *"Halt! Halt!"* the shout was repeated. All heads were turned to the gate. All motion had come to a stop. Only Lutek moved doggedly on, his barrel aloft on his shoulder, as though nothing were happening. And if Lutek did not stop neither would he, shouts or no shouts. Lutek was David's only salvation and he must be close to him now when every second counted. Let the German come. He'll seize him in his arms as though with a steel ring and hold him until Lutek grabbed the barrel with the

120

child and ran. With him they can do what they please, but they will not get David. A feeling of lion-strength surged through him with this resolve; and while all the others stood still he and Lutek moved toward their usual meeting place behind the pump.

No sooner had they put their barrels down on the ground when a rifle shot rang out in the air like a sharp clap of thunder. An audible gasp went up from those around the pump, their eyes glued to the gate. Little David was wide awake, his face contorted with fright; any moment he would break out into a wail. Lutek grabbed the barrel with the child and hoisted it up on his shoulder. No one but Hershel saw him walk away from the pump with quick determined steps and disappear into the hallway of the house across the street.

Hershel moved over to one of the Jews at the pump. "What happened?" he asked in a low voice.

"The guard shot a boy."

"Shot a boy?" Hershel muttered, as though in a daze.

"Even a deaf one could have heard it," the other said, with annoyance. "There, he's bringing him back. Can't you see?"

Yes, he could see. It was his friend, the policeman, who was carrying the boy's limp figure back to the gate. He was still a block away. The boy had run that far! One more second and perhaps he would have made it. But why had the boy chosen this gate? The children who made a dash for the Aryan side to beg for food usually did it through the main gate where there was much more activity, and the chances of sneaking past the guards were better than here. And of all days to have chosen this day! A religious Jew might read some higher meaning into this; he, Hershel, saw nothing but chance. Pure, blind chance.

And it could easily have been the other way around. Had the boy hesitated one more minute before making his dash for freedom little David might have saved his life. For by then the policeman would have done what he was supposed to do, offer the guard a cigarette and light it for him, and the boy's escape would have eluded the guard's notice.

When Hershel returned to the hospital and described to Lena what happened, she burst into tears. She cried for joy that her son made it and cried for sorrow that another's son didn't.

Two days later the following item appeared in the *Gazette & Courier* and ran for three days: "On the morning of May 12, 1942, a male infant was left on the doorstep of Pan and Pani Tadeusz Bielowski, 242 Pienkna Street. The rightful parents are requested to come to the above address to claim their child."

Afterword

"There were still very few people on the street when I came out with my child. I was holding her small hand fast in mine and was overcome by conflicting emotions. A thought crossed my mind: This may be the last walk you take with your little daughter. A voice replied: But you are leading her to life! If you do not manage to survive, at least you have lived a good portion of your life. You had beautiful and happy years. When your time comes you will depart with the comforting thought that you have saved your child. At any rate, you have done everything possible to save her. She must live. She has not yet tasted life; and only because she was born a Jewish child is it decreed that she must perish. So, despite the evil world, despite the 'New World Order,' she must live."

This was how one father remembered those emotion-filled moments when he led his eight-year-old daughter Margaret to the Warsaw Ghetto gate where the guards, who had been bribed in advance, were to look the other way when she crossed over to the Aryan side. The child was equipped with a new, Polish-sounding name and an address of a Polish "aunt" with whom she was to stay. She knew that from the moment she set foot on the other side of the gate she was never to betray, by either word or act, her Jewish identity.

That little girl was one of the few fortunate children whose parents had succeeded, with the aid of some courageous Polish humanitarians, to find a Polish family to take her in, and were able to procure the necessary funds demanded for her shelter and upkeep. Most parents in this and other ghettos had neither the right contacts with the outside world nor the enormous sums *of money required to buy shelter for a Jewish child. According to the Warsaw Ghetto chronicler, Emmanuel Ringelblum, the price was "around 100 zlotys per day and half a year's payment demanded in advance for fear that the parents might, in the meantime, be deported. To settle a child on the Aryan side required tens of thousands of zlotys. . . . . Destitute parents had to witness, with pain-constricted hearts, how their children were the first victims of the various selections and [deportation] actions."*

Some Poles became attached to the Jewish children they sheltered and when they learned that the children's parents had perished, adopted them. Others, when payment ceased, turned the children out into the streets to fend for themselves. Sooner or later these children were picked up by Polish or German police and returned to the ghetto where they were then first in line for the next deportation.

But money was not the only obstacle to saving Jewish children. Some churches and Polish orphanages were willing to take a limited number of ghetto children for a more accessible fee than that demanded by those Poles who looked upon the sheltering of Jews as a money-making proposition. But the prerequisites for taking the children became another obstacle, in many instances an insurmountable one.

These institutions would take only boys and girls with a "good appearance" which meant children who did not look Jewish, and boys who were not circumcised. Circumcision was a telltale sign of Jewishness. There were very few non-circumcised boys in the ghetto. These restrictions severely limited the number of children who could have been saved. Some children who had already made the hazardous journey from the ghetto to the institution were rejected for not meeting the physical qualifications and were returned to the ghetto. Ringelblum's own ten-year-old son was one of them.

Some ghetto children, caught in a deportation action with their parents or alone, managed to leap from the train that was taking them to one of the death camps.

If the young escapees were lucky enough not to be hit by the bullets fired at them by the German or Ukrainian guards who accompanied the train, they had another chance at the struggle for survival in a world lurking with dangers all around them.

Little Margaret was one of the fortunate ones whose parents survived the Holocaust and who were reunited with them after the war. Many Jewish children who had been sheltered in private homes and orphanages or, posing as Christians, had fended for themselves on the Aryan side as cigarette vendors, boot-blacks or singing beggars, never saw their parents again.

As the war ground to a halt and Jewish committees sprang up in liberated areas to begin the rehabilitation of survivors, they let it be known that they were ready to receive all orphaned Jewish children and compensate their Polish guardians for their upkeep. With the aid of the government, and assistance from the Joint Distribution Committee of America and other Jewish aid societies, a number of children's homes were set up in various parts of Poland where the orphans lived under the solicitous care and guidance of dedicated staffs.

One such children's home was in Pietrolesiu, a small town in Lower Silesia. It was named after the famous educator and children's writer Janusz Korczak who, in August 1942, was deported to the death camp, Treblinka, together with the 200 children from the Warsaw Ghetto orphanage of which he was the director. Here, among the boys and girls ranging from tiny tots to sixteen-year-olds, were some miracles of survival— children who had been snatched from the ovens of Maidanek in the last hours of the war. The German military truck speeding them to their death had been overtaken by the advancing Red Army. The driver and the SS guards abandoned the vehicle with its human cargo and fled. Thus the children were saved.

Not all reunions between children and surviving parents went smoothly. Some Polish guardians had become so attached to their Jewish wards that they adopted them, thinking that their parents had perished. At the end of the war, when the parents showed up, they were reluctant to return them. And there were instances where children, having been raised as Christians and in an anti-Semitic atmosphere, refused to be identified as Jews, rejecting their Jewish parents. This was particularly true in cases where the child was separated from its parents when it was very young and had little or no recollection of them. In some such cases it took the intervention of the law and a dramatic court battle before the child was returned to its rightful parents.

One story recorded in Holocaust documents is very similar to the story of little David. It tells of an uncircumcised infant boy who was taken in for shelter by a young Polish couple. For the child's and the couple's own safety, and with the approval of the parents, it was announced in the press that he was a foundling and later adopted.

The parents survived the war, and when they came to claim their son, now nearly five years old, it was not the guardians who raised objections but the boy. He insisted that the Poles were his real parents and that he, too, was a Pole and not a Jew. To lessen the trauma of the child's abrupt separation from the people he loved and regarded as his true parents, the Polish couple agreed to move in with the Jewish couple and live together until the boy showed his acceptance of his true parents. When the boy began to call the Polish woman "auntie" and the Jewish woman "mother," they knew it was time to move. The two couples continued to visit each other and remained friends.

In that sorrowful and anguish-laden period this was one of the few stories with a happy ending. Maybe it was also the ending to the story of little David.

About the Author

Yuri Suhl came to the United States as a young immigrant from Poland. He attended City College and New York University.

Mr. Suhl has written several volumes of Yiddish poetry and a number of books in English. Among the latter are: *One Foot in America* (a novel); *They Fought Back* (the factual account of Jewish resistance to Nazi slaughter); a biography of Ernestine Rose; *Simon Boom Gives a Wedding* (a picture book for young children); and *An Album of Jews in America*.

At present, Mr. Suhl divides his time between writing, teaching, and sculpting with found objects. He and his wife live in New York City.

AVON 🔷 NEW LEADER IN PAPERBACKS

CONTEMPORARY READING FOR YOUNG PEOPLE

☐ Blackbriar William Sleator	22426	$ .95
☐ Don't Look and It Won't Hurt Richard Peck	30668	1.25
☐ Dreamland Lake Richard Peck	30635	1.25
☐ The Enchanted Elizabeth Coatsworth	24257	.95
☐ Go Ask Alice Alice	21964	1.25
☐ A Hero Ain't Nothin' but a Sandwich Alice Childress	20222	.95
☐ It's Not What You Expect Norma Klein	32052	1.25
☐ The Loners Nancy Garden	20230	.95
☐ Mary Dove Jane Gilmore Rushing	22756	.95
☐ Mom, the Wolfman and Me Norma Klein	18259	.95
☐ Please Don't Go Peggy Woodford	20248	.95
☐ Run William Sleator	32060	1.25
☐ Soul Brothers and Sister Lou Kristin Hunter	28175	1.25
☐ A Teacup Full of Roses Sharon Bell Mathis	20735	.95
☐ Through a Brief Darkness Richard Peck	21147	.95